Music of Maninjau

David Green

Published by bluechrome publishing 2006

2 4 6 8 10 9 7 5 3 1

Copyright © David Green 2006

David Green has asserted his right under the Copyright, Designs and Patents Act 1988 to be identified as the author of this work.

This book is sold subject to the condition that it shall not, by way of trade or otherwise, be lent, resold, hired out, or otherwise circulated without the publisher's prior consent in any form of binding or cover other than that in which it is published and without a similar condition including this condition being imposed on the subsequent purchaser.

All the characters in this book are fictitious and any resemblance to actual persons, living or dead is purely coincidental.

First published in Great Britain in 2006 by
bluechrome publishing
PO Box 109,
Portishead, Bristol. BS20 7ZJ
www.bluechrome.co.uk

A CIP catalogue record for this book is available from the British Library.
ISBN   1-904781-35-7
This book was edited and prepared for print by
Associated Writing, Editing and Design Services

www.awed-services.com

Acknowledgements

Special thanks to Pi-Goong Warutama for providing inspiration and to my family and friends for their love and support.

Also, my thanks go to Ken Methold and Pat and Paul Mitchell at the Capricorn Hill Writer's Retreat, to the Purdie family, in whose home the adventure began and to Anthony Delgrado and John F Griffiths for their support and patience.

The idea for this book was inspired by the passage relating to the death of the Music Master in *The Glass Bead Game* by Herman Hesse.

Contents

Prologue

Part 1: Musica Instrumentalis

Part 2: Musica Humana

Part 3: Musica Mundana

Music of Maninjau

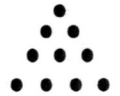

Prologue

Bones. Feathers. Fabric on the walls. The tears of a young girl falling on an old man's cheek. Chanting, singing, the stamping of feet. Pots of burning herbs, sticks of incense. She cradles his head in her arms, soothing him with whispers. Drums are thumping nearby. He looks up with half-blind eyes.
'Chenoa?' He rasps.
'Pilan?'
The pitter-patter of tears.
'Do you have them?'
'Yes.'
'Keep them and find me.'
'I will find you.'
'You will find me.'
'Sleep, Innie. Sleep and be still.'
'Find me.'

His lips move but the voice has emptied of breath. A candle fizzles. The drumming turns to echoes.

Part 1 – Musica Instrumentalis

Flux. Noise

The aircraft is cruising at thirty-three thousand feet. I'd been bumped up to business class, the unexpected but pleasant result of arriving late after a frenetic dash through the capital. England is flooded. Trains are learning to swim and the people will soon learn to breathe water. In time the landscape will change irreversibly.

A month ago I was still at my desk delivering ultimatums to unscrupulous landlords, drafting pointless reports and flirting with staff twice my age. Every morning I fell into the underworld of London Transport and emerged an hour later bedraggled, rat-like, clawing my way into the office to count the pendulous procession of hours. The shock subsided by noon, but the same rhythms took hold when five o'clock came and the underworld swallowed me once more: the sliding whine of the doors and the bustle of hundreds of scrambling feet. A change was inevitable.

Varanasi is drifting by below. In a blanket of pitch black I imagine I can see the dim flicker of lantern flames, streetlights shining like watery stars. I wonder what the people are doing. Is anyone wondering what is happening up here? A planeload of strangers hurtling towards the transport hub of South East Asia: Bangkok, Krung Thep – the City of Angels, the city of sin in the land of smiles.

I'm shifting in my seat. We're over the Bay of Bengal. The sun is rising again. The corners of the Earth are dyed red.

It was five o'clock in the morning when the wheels struck the tarmac and we disembarked. I collected my baggage and drifted through customs like a wraith. When the doors to the airport opened, the full impact of the smothering heat struck. Some staggered as it hit them, involuntarily stepping back into the air-conditioned arrivals lounge. Others walked on, oblivious. I stood by the taxi rank and savoured the strange and strangling air. I held my arms out so that the heat could penetrate me, so no part of me was left susceptible to shock later on. It was only five in the morning and Bangkok was still warming up. Cars roared past, dogs bayed in the distance, insects buzzed. I lit a cigarette and before I knew it, I was in a taxi.

Like all first-time arrivals in the city, I ended up on the Khao Sarn Road with its garish neon signs, surrounded by human driftwood and the all-consuming stench of garbage and money changing hands. Mangy dogs patrolled the streets, scratching themselves blind while students from all around the world did the same thing with alcohol. I bought a beer and a packet of cigarettes and buried my senses in the city, drinking myself into a stupor with a host of strangers whilst trying to acclimatise to the suffocating heat. When the bars lost their appeal, I went further afield. I spent days on the canals, on the *khlong* boats, roaring through filthy water littered with turtle corpses and the scurrying tails of panicking rats. Toothless old men watched from their makeshift huts. Children trod water frantically in their efforts to both wave and stay afloat.

Waking up with a hangover on the seventh day after my arrival, I decided to leave. I had no idea where to go, no plan whatsoever. I wandered into a travel agent and picked the name of a town at random from a list of destinations on a tattered board: Penang, Malaysia. Before I knew it, I had the ticket in my hand and the agent had my money. I was leaving Thailand already.

I spent my last day in Bangkok recovering from a week of alcohol abuse and the lethal effects of *Krongthip* cigarettes, finding solace in the cushions of the guesthouse sofas. As my fingers rolled across the fret board of my guitar, my thoughts turned back to London. Life there had been frustrating. Music – so often a lifeline in difficult times – had been equally frustrating. The process of musical creation is an expression of an inner yearning. The pursuit of beauty in music is the act of drowning in this yearning, allowing one's self to be consumed by a nostalgia for something indescribable, shadowy and indistinct. It's like feeling homesick when you're already safe at home. The melodies might resonate with a sense of sadness or loss, but they had always delivered solace and reassurance. When they failed to do this, frustration crept in and I grew ill. I couldn't even tune a guitar: no note sounded true and the strings always clashed. I felt fractured inside. During a bout of fever that lasted several weeks and left me in a fragile state for months afterwards, I began a journal that I still carry with me. In the hours before I left Bangkok, I read through it. Much of it was written in a delirious state, some of it was barely comprehensible, but pockets of clarity were scattered here and there.

> *Music: the human spirit has always pined for it. Before we could talk we intuitively knew the patterns of rhythm. Before we filled a heaven with gods, we developed the sacred art of music by which we could worship them. Why did men beat bones upon the rocks? To be heard? To have a voice in the*

> *vast and isolating universe? Did the syncopated beats of nature seek out the soul of man?*

Through my wretched bouts of fever, I had perceived an ether permeated by a fundamental harmony, a rippling universal vibration that set everything into motion.

> *Everything in the vast and sprawling splendour of creation is imbued with a rhythm, a fundamental vibration, an echo of a noise that permeates all space and time.*
>
> *The universe is a dynamic rush of excited noise and light, a seething cauldron of matter and energy, forever caught up in a violent state of flux. Nothing can be absolutely still; nothing can cease to vibrate. Vibration is sound.*

In my delirium I had imagined that musical instruments were tools to tap into this ubiquitous ether, translating strange mappings of perfection into languages that we could more easily rationalise and understand.

> *Flux. Noise. And from the chaos, harmony and concord.*

I read the description of my fevered dreams four or five times before I put the journal away and set off towards the station. I suppose I was looking for clues. In Asia, with enough money to last me for a year, I could try to gain a clearer understanding of my frustrations. At the very least, I could rekindle my passion for music.

On my way through the city, I stopped at a bookshop to find something to occupy me during the journey. I found a battered tome of Chinese poetry. The I Ching was buried somewhere in the depths of my rucksack and I thought they'd complement each other, so I bought the book and headed on to the Hualamphong station. At midnight I boarded the train for Penang.

I gave up trying to sleep. A child was crying in the next compartment. A mosquito was buzzing somewhere. For a while I tried to identify the note of its wings, but I couldn't pin it down. I opened my newly-acquired book at a random page, saw the word 'music' and began reading. The author's name was Lu Bu We, but no other information was provided.

> *The origins of music lie far back in the past. Music arises from Measure and is rooted in the Great Oneness. The Great Oneness begets the two Poles; the two Poles beget the power of Darkness and Light.*

When capital letters are used on otherwise ordinary words, deeper meanings are usually implied, but I didn't understand the references to *Measure* and *Poles* and the *Great Oneness*. Why and how does music arise from *Measure*? And how was it rooted in the begetter of darkness and light?

> *Music is founded on the harmony between Heaven and Earth, on the concord of brightness and obscurity.*

The train rolled on through the darkness of the tropical peninsular, passing through towering limestone mountains and dense jungles that eventually gave way to endless rice plains. The soporific rhythm of the wheels soothed my mind. I put the book aside and slept until the train screeched to a halt at our destination. The passengers diffused like clouds of smoke in the heat of the Malaysian morning. I gathered my belongings and headed for the ferry.

In George Town I found a room and then went out for a meal in the market square. In the afternoon I wandered around the shopping quarter, imbibing the atmosphere, drifting in and out of curio shops. When the early evening downpour came I ducked into the nearest one. It was filled with oriental paraphernalia and junk. I came across a set of small tablets in a glass case that were inscribed with a musical mantra on the theme of good and evil. I was fascinated by the delicate symbols so I asked if I could watch him inscribe one for me. He agreed and led me through a curtain into another room.

A small table held a set of knives, inks and brushes, and a stock of stone tablets. He sat down and started to mark the tiny characters on a tablet with graceful fingers, completely absorbed. His back was bent in a permanent stoop and his body was frail, but his eyes maintained a fiery spark. He was calm and careful, like a grandfather who has worked on the land for a lifetime. The candle flames flickered on the blade of the knife as it danced under his command. When I glanced away from his work, I noticed that the other end of the room was filled with instruments. The shadows they cast seemed to be moving in time with his knife, imbuing the strange shapes with a lithe animal quality. I stared for a while, convinced the instruments themselves were moving, but they were not. Turning my attention back to the old man, I asked if he was a musician. He nodded. I noticed another table that was covered with tools and a profusion of strings, bellows, mouthpieces, pedals and picks. I assumed that he either repaired or built the instruments I saw on the walls. I was intrigued, but became distracted as my mind recalled the words of Lu Bu We. I asked if the good and evil of the pendant inscription were like darkness and light. His back straightened a little, his eyes lifted from his work, and the knife stilled. He must have been surprised by my question, or perhaps by the foreknowledge apparent in my tone.

'Could be,' he said in a soft voice, without turning his head. The knife flickered and the candle flame glinted in his eyes. I abandoned subtlety and asked him bluntly if he knew who Lu Bu We was. His back straightened again and he turned with a bemused look. 'Why do you ask?'

'Because I've been reading his work.'

He appeared doubtful. I told him about the book from the shop in Bangkok and after a brief pause he smiled and motioned me to a chair. He was suddenly more voluble and inquisitive. I think he was both surprised and excited by my interest in him and his work. What had brought me here? Who was I with? Where had I come from? He stopped working on the pendant. I answered his questions as well as I could and he told me about his life: his family in China, a photograph of a young woman with two small children, edges frayed and colours faded. In George Town he lived alone, but he was always busy. He said he had many friends.

Though I was enjoying myself, I wanted him to answer my question, so I told him about my fevered dreams. I must have sounded like a lunatic. I thought at best he would simply humour me, but instead he became more serious and solemn. I sensed he was dancing around me, presumably withholding an answer until he knew more about me. When he eventually decided to respond, I struggled to keep up with the flurry of words. He spoke near-perfect English, but at a pace that blurred the consonants into vowels. He said that he had sacrificed wealth, family and friendship to fulfil the ambition that had taken over his life: he was reinterpreting the principles of Taoism. He claimed that the ancient text of the Tao-te-Ching was intended to be a doctrine of fundamental music and that the Lao-Tzu masterpiece had been misinterpreted for centuries. It was astonishing and improbable, but I felt a prickle of excitement. He was waiting for me to react, so I prompted him to continue. He asked me if I had read the Tao-te-Ching, and I said I had, but when I was too young to fully comprehend.

to fully comprehend.

To understand any work of philosophy, he explained, one must begin by understanding the words that describe the ideas. Every philosophy has its own idiosyncratic dictionary, its own language within which familiar and commonly used words have attenuated meanings. Once the nuances of the language are thoroughly understood, one must transcend the meaning of the words to gain insight. Words will lead you to the threshold of wisdom, he told me, but they're too heavy to carry you across. A true philosopher resides in an intuitive, boundless state, but a novice must start at the beginning – with words. He described the origins of yin and yang and the Tao and told me to reassess the words of Lu Bu We in the light of his explanations. That night, in my room, I was able to recall and write down a summary of his words.

> *Tao (the 'ridgepole'): The fundamental postulate, the 'great primal beginning' of all that exists – 't'ai chi' in its original meaning.*
>
> *The ridgepole is the simplest construct of form after the point: a line. The line represents the condition of 'oneness' prevalent in Chinese thought. It has the immediate effect of creating duality: up and down, left and right, light and dark, good and evil, matter and energy. The physical manifestation of the universe is based on this concept of fundamental duality. The continual flux between the two extreme forces gives rise to the phenomenal world.*
>
> *Earlier Chinese philosophers used the symbol of the circle: a symbol of both paradox and perfection: a line with neither beginning nor end; the great primal beginning - Tao.*
>
> *Yin/Yang: The fundamental opposites; the extreme forces. The combination of the circle and the line led to the classic yin/yang symbolism with the duality of light and dark em-*

ployed to represent the fundamental duality. The yin/yang symbol depicts both the 'oneness' in the universe and the opposites fundamental to the physical existence of the universe – the source of all change in the natural world.

It was difficult to take all of this in and simultaneously apply it to the words of Lu Bu We, but one thing was clear: his words were imbued with a higher level of relevance. *Music is rooted in the Great Oneness*; music is placed in the realm of the ridgepole, the unearthly, the ineffable. It is fundamental in nature, existing preternaturally in the great primal beginning. It is t'ai chi. It is Tao. *The Great Oneness begets the two poles.* I still didn't fully comprehend the implications. If I didn't understand Tao, what could I possibly learn from connecting the essence of music to it? For that matter, what did I know about 'the essence of music'?

I was impressed by the old man's sincerity and his self-belief. I had such a clear memory of his final words, spoken in near perfect English, that I was able to write them down verbatim.

He (Lu Bu We) was trying to say that music is founded in the fundamental harmony that lies behind the chaos of duality. The physical world we live in is a world of opposites, of contrasts and extremes: yin and yang; obscurity and brightness; heaven and earth; light and dark. But they're all just words we use, labels for the fundamental opposites. The important thing to remember is that music does not reside in the realm of duality, that is to say, in the manifestation of change that is the phenomenal world – its roots are ethereal. Its roots are Tao.

Were these the words I had travelled such a great distance to hear, the reason why I had given everything up in London? I was excited, but it was getting late and the old man had stopped talking and abruptly returned to his work. I waited in silence, my mind racing.

When he finished the pendant, he made a pot of tea and asked me more questions about my travels, my home and my plans. He showed me his instruments, letting me try some, but he refused to be drawn further on the subject of music. I felt it was time to leave, so I thanked him, paid him and said goodbye. I resolved to return and continue our conversation another day. As I pushed open the heavy doors and looked out at the seedy back streets of George Town, he took my arm, thanked me and spoke again.

'You might think me an eccentric old man with funny ideas, but there is truth in what I say – the fundamental melody is no myth. It is always there, humming softly in the fabric of the world. If you learn to hear it, well…' A light rain began to fall as he spoke.

'The perfect rhythm, the golden cosmic note,' I whispered without thinking.

'What?'

'*I'd find the perfect rhythm, the golden cosmic note; the one they made in heaven, the one the Angels wrote.* It's a line from a poem I wrote down once after waking with it in my head.' The ensuing silence went on for some time until the sudden movement as I flicked my wet hair aside seemed to stir the old man.

'Wait here. I must fetch something.' He went back into the shop and left me on the cold kerbside with the quiet hum of the bug-infested neon streetlights and the pouring rain. I rolled the pendant around in my fingers, leaning against the wall and looking up and down the empty street until the big doors swung open once more. 'I want you to have this one.' He held out another pendant. I started to refuse, but he insisted, snatching the original from my grasp and pressing the new one into my hand. 'No, do not refuse an old man. It is late; I am tired and I must go to bed. Call again if you are passing and don't get too wet on your way home. Goodbye!'

I realised that I hadn't asked his name. As the doors slammed shut, I looked at the new pendant and saw it was inscribed with exactly the same couplet as the one he'd taken from me. It looked identical. Standing in the sudden silence, bemused by his abrupt departure, I noticed a mark upon the panels of the heavy doors that seemed oddly familiar – a triangle of dots: one, two, three, then four. I stared at them, trying to recall where I'd seen them before, but I couldn't place them.

Ambling down the back alleys of the colonial town, my mind was alive with ideas. Things I had read came back in blurry paraphrases. I remembered the mythical 'music of the spheres', the harmony of heavenly bodies, inaudible to our ears. I pondered over the nature of subsonic and supersonic sound: an infinite landscape of noise that passes us by. I tried to imagine what it would be like to hear the continual quantum popping of matter becoming light, light becoming matter in a boundless spray of nanoscopic sound.

Flux. Noise, and from the chaos...

The whirr of the jungle cicadas has rhythms and beats that occur over timescales too small for us to perceive. Our brains are the most developed of all species, but the elaborate melodies of birdsong will always elude us. By the same token, we can never see the world through the eyes of a bat, or smell it like a dog. The details will always be lost to us.

Music is in all growing things;
And underneath the silky wings

*Of smallest insects there is stirred
A pulse of air that must be heard;
Earth's silence lives, and throbs, and sings.*

The world is full of music we can't hear.

When I returned to my room, I wrote down as much of the old man's words as I could remember. The ideas resonated with an intuition that had grown within me over years, but they were too esoteric, their connections vague and shapeless. Feeling compelled to act, but having no clear objective, I spent hours contemplating the sounds of the city streets: the hum of electricity, the dripping of rain, the squeal and purr of petrol engines, the pitter-patter of cicadas and the comedy gulp of the geckos. Eventually the sounds faded and I fell into sleep.

The next day I awoke with a renewed sense of enthusiasm. I rushed breakfast, returned to my room, and spent the whole day with my guitar, playing single notes, coupling them, playing triads, combining notes in all the ways I could think of. I went through hundreds of chords, shifting the mood with intervals I'd never dreamt of playing before. In the evening I found a piano in an empty bar and I did the same thing. For days I sat in front of the keys, but still I wasn't content. In the end I found myself striking single notes and listening intently to the fading echoes of the overtones. I tuned the strings of the guitar until they snapped. I replaced them and retuned them. The tragic words of Beethoven flashed through my head: 'It is, and always will be, a disappointing instrument'. He had commissioned the greatest piano makers of his time to design and build pianos, but the sounds could never match the music that rang sonorously through his subconscious.

With bitter disappointment, I left the instruments and began to meditate. I heard cars screeching through the rain-soaked streets, drunks yelling, street vendors heckling, dogs barking and the animal sounds of sex from the next room. I was becoming depressed. The depression developed into a form of despair and I ventured back towards the pendant engraver's shop in the hope that he could tell me more – anything to resolve my mood. I retraced my steps until the heavy doors were in front of me again. The first hint of something amiss was the absence of the pattern of dots upon the door. Somebody had scratched them away. I knocked: nothing. I knocked again: still nothing. I pushed gently and the doors swung open. I called out: nothing. I walked in hesitantly and found a silent house filled with empty boxes. An eerie stillness hung in the air. The furniture was beginning to accumulate dust – more dust than I would expect after only a few days' neglect. I walked through every room in the house and found no trace of the old man, the instruments or the pendants. There was nothing remotely familiar, just dust and empty boxes. I began to feel claustrophobic and left. In the streets my head began to spin as I tried to make sense of it. I walked up and down the road several times to check I was in the same place. When the rains returned, I ran back to my room, packed my bags, stuffed the bin with my broken strings and headed towards the station. Drops of rain hammered down. The crash of a wooden palette hitting the floor was like a blow on the side of my head. Motorbikes roared like jungle beasts and the cloth of my trouser leg scraped on my shoe like sandpaper. My heart thumped in my chest.

I boarded a train, retreated into my sleeping bag and woke up the next day back in Bangkok.

Thon

I bought a motorbike and drove north. I went from place to place, playing covers in bars for free beer and with different people every night. When the frenetic pace of the tourist haunts overwhelmed me, I veered from the beaten track and took refuge in the winding roads of the quiet countryside, finding secluded spots in which to meditate and take stock. The solitude drove me inwards but my mind was filled with noise and clutter and I couldn't bear to be alone. It was never long before I returned to the bars and clubs, where the hollow warmth of the audience's applause echoed the superficial familiarity that fellow travellers share. Rice wine, Chang Beer and cigarettes were my real friends. I was drifting. My eyes were slowly glazing over with each and every town or city I passed through, but I didn't notice. I'd lost interest. I didn't care.

When I tired of Thailand, I sold the bike, headed into Laos and cruised the sludgy Mekong in slowboats. The continuous roar of the engines eventually unsettled me and I took a speedboat further north. Days and weeks disappeared in the opium dens that straddle the Burmese and Chinese borders. I found a semblance of routine in those isolated tribal villages. Each day I woke up after noon, shovelled some nutrition into my dry mouth and trudged from the guesthouse to one of the huts on the outskirts. I offered strangers handfuls of notes and they gave me lost time in return. If I outstayed my welcome or grew weary of my surroundings, I staggered to another hut or another village. Eventually I found the Mekong again and I rode it all the way out of Laos.

In Cambodia, I headed straight for the magnificence of Angkor, convinced that the majestic splendour of the place would infuse me with direction and lift my spirits. I spent a week wandering through the mystifying synergies of tree and rock, admiring the twisting parasitic giants that had somehow fused with the boulders and bricks in strange and beautiful ways. Every morning I watched the sun rise from the shattered ruins of the temple of Prohm Bakhaeng. In the evenings I'd sometimes climb to the top of Angkor Wat, up the steep and narrow steps that force you to walk sideways. Other times I headed into the jungle on my own and found solitary, crumbling towers with gentle faces of Buddhas decaying in the creeping vines. I felt more at peace than I had done for a long time, but I remained restless. The pendant was still hanging around my neck, for some reason reminding me that I had left London with a purpose. Every time I rubbed it between my thumb and my finger, I thought about the engraver who had excited me with his words before disappearing without trace, turning my enthusiasm into a deepening sense of frustration.

On the outskirts of Phnom Penh, I placed my hands palm down on the killing fields and tried to imagine the terrifying ordeals of the innocent victims who had died there. Men, women and children were torn apart and destroyed in waves of violent madness. Their blood had turned to grass, but I couldn't sense their pain with my hands or my heart. I went to the nearby firing range and fired the same weapons that may have ended their lives, but even the crack and roar of the rifles did not stir me. The city itself was peppered with craters in the roads, festering mounds of decomposing refuse and rubble, disfigured street-beggars and occasional burnt-out cars. Nothing touched me.

I moved on, passed through Sihanoukville and returned to Thailand. In the Gulf of China I waded out a hundred metres from the shore and watched as storm clouds enveloped the island, rendering it almost invisible. Lightning crashed, thunder roared, the rain smashed into the water like shards of glass as I stood waist-high in the ocean and watched it unfold. I should have been filled with joy and fear. I felt neither.

My life was a constant wheel of change. Every day brought something I had never known before, but no matter how incredible or mind-shattering the experience, nothing could cut through the numbness. I travelled for weeks, months, maybe even years. Not a single day went by without a fleeting thought for the engraver. I held an image of him in the periphery of my mind, and every so often, I'd turn to him and expect something. My health began to slide. I started eating badly. I drank too much and smoked too much. I decided to return to Chiang Mai, so I bought another bike and once again headed north. I met Thon on the night I arrived.

It was late, and I was wandering the back alleys with a bottle of beer when I heard the most remarkable sounds emanating from an open-fronted cafe-bar several hundred yards ahead of me. I was drawn in by what sounded like several guitars being played beautifully. The bar was very busy but the clientele was surprisingly still and quiet, entranced by the performers, who I couldn't see from where I was standing. It was too busy to get any closer, so I stood at the back and listened. When I closed my eyes I saw melodies dancing around each other, shooting out like jets of flame around a centre, curling around upon themselves and ebbing to their natural resolution. I was captivated. Someone bumped into me, and when I opened my eyes I could see the stage. There was only one man with two hands and one guitar. It was Thon, though I didn't know his name at the time. His performance was as captivating to watch as it was to hear. His forearms, wrists and fingers danced behind a veil of black hair that cascaded from his forehead and hid parts of the instrument. I looked around and noticed everyone was mesmerised. His talents were striking; his music beyond description. He played for another half-hour, then the bar subsided into drunken revelry, more in keeping with a Friday night in the tourist quarter of Chiang Mai. Before I could gather my senses, he had gone. I was stunned by what I'd experienced; I had to find him. I returned the next night but again, he left before I could speak to him, because I hadn't noticed he'd stopped playing because his music lingered so vividly in my head. It was still there when I went to bed. It kept me from sleeping. On the third night I forced myself from my reverie during the last song, pushed through the crowd and made my way to his side. As he rose from his stool, I introduced myself and complimented him on his playing. He thanked me politely, but showed no interest, keeping his eyes on the guitar as he gently placed it in its case. He must have received compliments from drunken tourists all the time. Half of them probably woke up the next day with no recollection of his music. I asked him if he would consider playing with me, and he demurred. I offered him a drink, and he refused. I found myself alone again, standing helplessly by the bar like a lost dog. I drank, smoked, thought, drank some more and left.

On the fourth night, I arrived early and found myself a

seat next to the street. When he began to play I closed my eyes, and focussed entirely upon the notes. I forgot about trying to meet him and just enjoyed the music. I was impressed by the subtlety of his playing, by the dynamic multiplicity of his tones, by the various timbres he somehow managed to conjure from the six strings, but most of all, by the sheer depth of expression. I found myself murmuring an imagined lyric to the instrumental music, a melody of whispers. It was communication. When I opened my eyes the music had long since finished and Thon was standing over me, coughing, leaning on his guitar case with a cigarette hanging lazily in his fingers and his long black hair hiding half his face.

'You asked me yesterday if we could play sometime.' He spoke slowly and quietly in good English. I could barely hear him over the noise of the bar. I didn't reply; I was still listening to the last chord he'd played. 'We can meet here tomorrow afternoon if you like. I'm Thon. You?'

'Sebastian.'

'Hello, Sebastian. I'm in a hurry now, but I'll be here tomorrow at two. Okay?'

'I'll be here.'

And he left. I went back to the guesthouse a few minutes later, drank a pint of water and headed straight for bed.

The air is full of smoke but for some reason it doesn't hurt when I breathe. I can't feel myself breathing. I can't feel my ribs rising and falling. A hand is reaching out towards me through the cloudy blue atmosphere. It feels as if it is passing straight through me, but I can see it there in front of me. I try to reach out and take it, but no arm rises to my command. I have no arms because I am the smoke. *The hand will never reach me.*

At quarter to two the next day, I went to the bar. Thon arrived exactly at two. I offered to buy him a drink but he seemed restless and asked if I'd go for a walk. We made our way towards the empty Night Market and passed the time in idle conversation. He pointed out a good restaurant, warned me about another, told me to avoid a certain street at night, and showed me a temple he sometimes went to for meditation. After about fifteen minutes, he began asking me questions — about my family, my home, my past, my future, my dreams, ambitions, hopes and desires. I answered each question as fully and openly as I could. I was completely honest about my recent misadventures throughout South-East Asia, even though I felt a degree of shame when I talked of it. I kept two things from him: the mysterious engraver and my subsequent bout of madness in George Town. I also didn't go into any detail about the strange experiences I had had in London when the fever had hold of me. I didn't feel comfortable talking to anyone about these things, especially people I didn't know well enough to trust. By the time we reached his home an hour or so later, I felt he knew me reasonably well.

We sat and drank tea. He handed me one of his guitars and asked me to play. I was surprisingly nervous. I'd normally sing something in similar circumstances, but I didn't think it was appropriate on this occasion, so I finger-picked an instrumental piece I had composed in Cambodia. He listened and watched for a few minutes, then picked up another guitar and played with me. I struggled to keep time because I was listening intently to what he was playing. When the music came to an end, he invited me to be his guest, and from that moment, he became my teacher and my friend. We developed a daily routine. In the mornings we'd play music, usually for about four hours. In the afternoons, he visited friends and took care of his affairs while I'd usually go for walks, take the motorbike out to the nearby waterfalls or spend my time leafing through Thon's extensive library of notes and articles about music. We ate together in the early evening and afterwards spent an hour or so talking, drinking tea and cleaning our guitar strings. He cleaned his strings every day, and I too developed the habit. In the evenings we played in the bars. He played almost every night. I only played a few nights a week. I stopped playing covers altogether. I stopped drinking.

As the days went by we grew closer and he told me more about himself. He had grown up in Bangkok. His parents – like mine – had provided him with a good education and plenty of opportunities, but they had never taken the time to find out what made him tick; they had never accepted who he really was and what he wanted from life. His failure to communicate these things to them exacerbated the situation. They pushed him in directions that were unsuited to his nature, which caused heated arguments. Eventually, they rejected him altogether. His university fees were a farewell gift.

As a student he had become actively involved in popular left-wing political movements. He fell in with bad company and began associating with dangerous criminal elements in the capital. His student days culminated in a dramatic, near-fatal experience that he survived only because a taxi driver took him to the nearest hospital despite his protests. His health never fully recovered and he often fell into fits of coughing that wracked his body. Disillusioned and traumatised, he left the capital and lived alone in the mountains. A few years later he left Thailand and went to Canada to live with a girl named Nathalia. They'd originally met in Chiang Mai, instantly felt connected, and she had convinced him to abandon his hermetic lifestyle and spend the summer travelling with her. A year later, he accepted her invitation to go to

Canada. Though he spoke of her often, I never found out why their relationship came to an end, or why. She was a musician too, he told me, and it was through her that he developed his zeal for music. When he returned to Thailand he moved to Chiang Mai and made a living playing music. He taught as well, but only accepted one student at a time.

I tried to make the most of every hour we spent together. Each day brought a new revelation to my playing, new patterns for my fingers to trace, new rhythms to follow. I learnt more about harmony than I had ever imagined possible. My technique improved: my fingers moved faster and more fluidly over the frets, I thought less and played with more clarity, more honesty, more emotion. I started crying on one occasion. I didn't notice until one of the teardrops landed on a string. Despite all this, I was still frustrated and did not know why. I tried to ignore the feeling and hid it from Thon. I began to spend less time taking walks or riding out to the waterfalls and more poring over the contents of Thon's library. I found all kinds of weird and wonderful articles, most of which were not referenced and had no indication of authorship. One particular piece was so striking that I wrote it in my journal. I later found out that it was an extract from something Nathalia had written, an essay, or perhaps just part of a letter that had found its way into the library:

> *The way music changes over the years, the way it endlessly grows and expands to find new forms or reverts to develop afresh – so many different forms with different complexities, stranger, more intricate rhythms, more elaborated melodies... obscure and convoluted harmonies. It's all novelty, decoration, costume. Imagine yourself alone in a room with the greatest and most graceful dancer in the world. Her silhouette is like a river rolling through the room and every*

movement is a pure intimation of natural harmony; the air dances around the dancer who dances through the air. Every movement mystifies and astounds you with a supernatural sense of perfection. You sit for hours transfixed by her grace. You know that you have seen a thing of wild and natural beauty, like a tiger in hunt or an eagle gently rising. It moves you and you leave the room uplifted.

A week later you go to the theatre and the same dancer performs in a costume of brilliant reds and yellows. The lighting punctuates her form with subtle blues and greens. Tempestuous music spurs her on as she dances her way through a storyline with plot and character, intrigue and resolution. What affects you the most? The shape of her body in silhouette or the tragic denouement of one of the subplots? The grace of her movements or the programmatic contours of sounds? The details of colour and sound and story distract from the beauty of the thing itself; you inevitably leave the building with sadness and a sense that something pure has been devalued.

Music is like the dancer: no matter how much you embellish it with finery and tempestuous effects, no matter how cleverly you add the colour, the music remains the sole provider of true wonder, the 'beautiful thing'.

To truly appreciate music you must let it dance alone.

The words triggered a memory. Several months earlier I had been standing alone on a mountain in northern Laos as a thunderstorm was gathering. The sun was slowly setting and the sky above the mountains trailed through a spectrum of colours into the distance: dark skies of the storm behind me, clear blue above me, then yellow, orange, cherry-pink, and finally a deep, thick crimson that bled over the distant horizon. In the accumulating cloud I noticed an eagle spiralling on a vent of hot air, tracing circles many miles across as it rose ever higher towards the oncoming mantle of night. I stood transfixed, amazed that, in the absence of an artist, such phenomenal beauty could exist unframed and unnoticed by the galleries of London, Paris or New York. They display only representations of representations of things that aren't always beautiful to begin with.

I visited a zoo when I was in Malaysia. An eagle was there, trapped in a cage. Its wings were unfurled but it could not take leave of the earth and fly. All traces of beauty had been removed. The zookeepers had made the mistake of believing that the object itself was inherently beautiful, without realising the beauty lay in the eagle's spiralling through a spectrum of colours in a thunder-struck high-mountain skyline.

When Thon came back in the evening, I told him what I'd been thinking. He picked up his guitar, and as he was tuning up he said, 'In Ancient China, the quality of a single note was more important than melody or rhythm – perfection of tone was paramount.' He beckoned me to pick up my guitar and we played again. Music was our principle means of communication, subtler than words, more direct and emotive. One evening, the cacophony of the monsoon forced us to stop playing. We made tea and talked. He asked me again why I had come to Chiang Mai and I reiterated the tale of my debauched time in the wilderness in more detail, but I sensed that he suspected I was hiding something. I still didn't want to tell him about the engraver, and I didn't show him the pendant, though in retrospect I should probably have done both. I did tell him about the fever and the strange compulsion to wind up my life in London and leave England. As I spoke I was startled by the tenor and timbre of my words. I couldn't hide the frustrations that I still felt towards music and my life in general. Music, for him, was a religion, and the inherent mysteries and frustrations were mitigated by something akin to faith. Thon sensed my frustrations and treated them like an absence of faith. When he spoke, his voice acquired a new gravity. His health had been steadily improving since my arrival and he spoke more easily.

'I don't know why you feel this compulsion, Sebastian, or why you struggle with things that are straightforward. You are a good student, but you have much to learn. You need discipline and devotion, and I think you have them both. Sometimes people realise their path is music, and when they begin to walk they find they can look nowhere else, so consumed are they. When you meet these people you will know them.' His words appeared carefully-chosen and were seriously conveyed. This in itself was not unusual, but I couldn't help noticing that they seemed prepared, rehearsed. I suspected that there had been others like me. How many lost souls had he taken in to teach and inspire? I looked at him. His eyes were downcast. For a moment I was struck by how similar his expression and posture were to the old engraver: leaning over, back bent, eyes on the floor, deep in thought – an unusual posture for Thon. As if sensing my thoughts, he lifted his eyes, resumed his normal posture and said softly, 'Let me tell you about Nathalia.'

Rol-mo Rig-pa

'When I left Canada, Nathalia was finishing a degree in ethnomusicology,' Thon began. 'When she graduated, she planned to teach at the university, but came to visit me in Thailand first. We spent a few enjoyable weeks together. I expected her to go back to Canada, but she was unsettled and didn't want to. She didn't want to stay here either, so she packed her bag and set off on her own.' Thon held out a bundle of pages. Letters from Nathalia, he said. He pointed out a sheet for me to read – mostly trivial conversation. Then I caught the words: ...*I am in Eastern Tibet. I'm not going back. I'm going to do what we talked about in Chiang Mai...*

I asked him what it was they had talked about, but he ignored the question. 'That was the first letter I got. It came almost six months after she'd left. She must have travelled through Burma, even though I had warned her not to.' His eyes glazed. I waited. Eventually, Thon blinked, rubbed his face and continued. 'Nathalia studied the music of Tibet for her dissertation, so it made sense that she went there. She found a teacher, an old man who lived up in the mountains and made drums and flutes. She was always hungry to learn.' He passed me another sheet of paper.

...He was concentrating so hard he appeared to pay me no

> *attention. I don't know where my next thought came from, but it was very clear: the book he was working on was for me. He closed it, gently patting the cover like my grandfather used to pat my head. We didn't play that day, we stretched drum skins and talked. I didn't dare mention the book. He told me about the old music. I thought of you afterwards. I wrote it all down and have included it here.*

Thon didn't show me the next part of the letter, but he summarised it: 'Hidden behind the high wall of the Himalayas, the music of Tibet developed in isolation. The original ceremonial instruments used by Bon-po shaman priests were fashioned primarily from human remains: trumpets made from human thighbones and drums of human skulls. The deep resonance of ritual chanting projected an eerie quality of other-worldliness, intended to shift the levels of consciousness during practice. A sacred and highly evolved musical theory underpinned everything they did: the *Rol-mo Rig-pa*. Little remains of this semi-mythical Tibetan science of music, and what does remain is scattered in fragments. Most knowledge was passed down verbally. Some survived in the *Bardo Thodol*, meaning *Liberation by Hearing on the After-death Plane*, more commonly known as The Tibetan Book of the Dead.'

At first I presumed that the book mentioned in the letter must have been the *Rol-mo Rig-pa*, but Thon told me it wasn't. No full copies remained. It appeared that Nathalia's teacher was trying to reconstruct the ancient text, drawing on old parchments that had been passed down through his own family, a vast library of folklore that he kept in his memory, and – perhaps most importantly – his own innate musical sensitivities. The book was a work in progress.

He stared at another letter for a few moments, scanning

the page and clicking his tongue against the roof of his mouth. I waited patiently until he gave it to me.

...A terrible sense of foreboding churned my stomach as I made my way through the thick fog. When I eventually found his home I didn't waste time knocking on the door.

The hut was empty. I lit a lamp and gathered some kindling. As I was striking the flint, I caught sight of the leather-bound tome lying open on the floor with the flute across its pages. I shouted his name, but heard nothing but the wind whipping the walls. The flute was a glin-bu, very old. I'd not seen it before. I wrapped it in a piece of cloth, picked up the book and sat down at the table. I didn't want to open it, because it was his and he hadn't given it to me, but I couldn't help myself. I opened it and tried to read it, but the language was too obscure.

'There was nothing out of the ordinary about that day, except for the heavy fog,' Thon said, 'but by morning there was still no sign of the old man. Nathalia searched the hut for clues, but he had simply disappeared. He hasn't been seen since.' This seemed so similar to my own recent experience in Penang that I almost interrupted him. 'She was upset for a long time, but now she is working: reconstructing his instruments and translating the book. She's been writing more often recently, I look forward to her letters.'

'Has she told you what's in the book?'

'Read this. It is part of the last letter I received from her. I've highlighted the relevant bits.'

...so in antiquity the enlightened scholars of Tibet devised eight categories of instruments, each representing one of the eight inner sounds. These inner sounds were supposedly heard by the illuminated yogis in the deepest levels of yogic

> *trance meditation. They tried to find ways of reproducing the tranquil harmonies with instruments, and in so doing, devised the categories. Their final ambition was to find a way of accurately relaying the inner sounds to the ears of laypeople, offering anyone a 'sonic glimpse of nirvana'. According to what I've been able to decipher so far, if a listener is well-trained and sensitive enough, they should be able to perceive these fundamental harmonies without the need for yogic practices and deep meditation.*
>
> *(cf: The Hindu Aum: the theory of an elemental, primordial and omnipresent sound. Do you remember? It's supposed to ring in our ears from the moment we are born, continuing unnoticed until we die. We are so accustomed to its presence that we never even notice it is there.)*

I read the note two or three times. Thon picked up his guitar and began playing a gentle melody in a minor key, his eyes glazed like polished stone. He didn't look well and his breathing was awkward. I was lost in thought, buried beneath a surge of questions I wanted to ask. I needed to tell Thon about the engraver and his disappearance, the similarity with Nathalia's music teacher. I wanted to know more about the *Rol-mo Rig-pa*. I wanted to know what Nathalie and Thon had spoken about before she had left. It was late though, and I knew we'd not talk much more that night. Rain was clamouring on the roof and the teapot was drained. I lay back on my bed, listened to Thon's playing and fell asleep.

Next morning I woke early. Thon was already tending to the first pot of the day. I drank the tea he offered and took a few moments to mull over the questions I was determined to ask. I sensed the time still wasn't right. He could be very abrupt, but I had to remember that he suffered from a great deal of pain, which was often worse in the morning. I sat back and drank my tea, waking up slowly. It was then that he told me to leave. I thought he was joking, but it wasn't in his nature to make jokes of that kind. With one hand he took my empty teacup and with the other he gave me a map of Northern Thailand, with a cross marked in the Doi Inthanon National Park. He told me he often went there when the city suffocated him, that it was tranquil and calming. He told me I should go there, leaving as soon as possible. I couldn't think of any suitable reply. I knew the place. I'd gone there for the same reasons he gave – to get away from the world. The last time I'd been there I had taken a few bottles of Mekong whisky, a bag of local herbs and a girl from Israel who insisted on calling me Simon. I turned the map in my hands and noticed something scribbled on the back. He told me it was the address of a woman called Nam who lived in a town called Lamphun, saying that if I was nearby, I 'might like to pay her a visit'. She was an old friend. I was confused. I remember thinking that *nam* is the Thai word for water and no other thought could displace it. 'It is no longer right for you to be here – our paths may cross but they are not the same.' I nodded. My mouth was probably gaping, my eyes fixed on his. 'Have you ever heard of the '*chilla*'? It's a custom for Indian musicians to undergo a period of isolation with their instrument. The normal length is forty days, but...'

'Forty days!'

'...but I don't think you need take that long. It doesn't matter how long it takes, as long as you carry the spirit of the chilla into the time you spend alone. That is important.'

'Alone?'

He went on to tell me that devoted Indian musicians spend the chilla playing their instrument intensely, in isolation, only stopping to eat, drink, sleep and go to the toilet. They do so to reach a stage where they have exhausted every musical possibility they can conceive. If they persevere, they may go on to discover new modes of creativity, stretching their talent to previously unimagined levels, or they might lose their mind. The trauma can be so bad that many give up and become mendicants. Hallucinations and visions are considered normal. Traditionally, an Indian musician undertakes three chilla in a lifetime. I realised that in George Town I had undergone an approximation of a chilla. The few days I spent there had been enough to cause months of distraction, as Thon knew. Perhaps he was wary of insisting I undertake the full commitment.

'Do you still have your I Ching?'

'Yes.'

'Do you use it?'

'Not recently, no.'

'Take it with you and read from it each day. Perhaps it will help guide you. At the very least it will relax you. Don't worry too much about the words – just concentrate and be mindful when casting the sticks.'

'Okay.'

I was confused. Was I about to go into the wilderness for forty days? Alone?

'If you stayed here with me, you would become a fine musician. You would master your instrument and take great pleasure in playing it, but that might not be enough for you. I have no plans to leave, so if you need me I will be here.' His words immediately conjured up visions of empty boxes piled high in a room full of dust. It didn't make sense for me to leave. I was still learning. We enjoyed each other's company and very rarely, if ever, found the other's presence uncomfortable. So why was I leaving? And would I really see him again?

Ten minutes later I was waving from my motorbike,

backpack fastened to the seat and guitar strapped to my back. After turning a few corners, I stopped and switched the engine off, confused. I still wasn't fully awake. It wasn't far to Doi Inthanon, a few hours at the most, and I had nowhere else to go, nowhere to be. I kicked the starter and left Chiang Mai.

The Chilla

The heat of the motorbike hazed the air as it roared beneath me. I was back in the mountains of Northern Thailand, hurtling through the scenery that I had come to know so well: the swaying overhang of huge trees, the moist air of the valley floor, the sounds of stillness and life in the jungle. The light was as sharp as the contrast of colours, everything tinged with a greater lucidity through the yellow lenses of my sunglasses. I was free, sorry to have left Thon but glad to be away from the hectic bustle of the city. Here I could focus my thoughts and let them lead wherever they might. I was refreshed, alive.

I checked the map before heading off-road. A moonscape plateau sprawls out behind the peak of Doi Inthanon, the tallest rock in Thailand. The dense jungle gives way to a dusty profusion of small shrubs, dry and brittle in the glare of the sun and punctuated by clumps of trees. The place where Thon had directed me was easy to find, a small clearing surrounded by an irregular pentagon of trees that jutted from the undergrowth. I parked my motorbike against a tree, pitched the tent, strung the hammock, ate a little food and dozed.

I woke to the heat of the mid-afternoon sun and the healthy pressure of fresh thoughts. I had memories of before: playing music, performing to emptiness, with only the chink of whisky bottles for percussion. I had memories of being inspired, but mostly I remembered the hollow embrace of a stranger, a smothering loneliness, blurred recollections formed in a mental haze. This time my mind was clear. No herbs, no bottles, empty or otherwise.

Music is the play of light on a ripple of water, the fluttering melodies of wind through trees.

I took the chilla seriously, beginning each day with several hours of flowing meditation and relaxation, allowing my thoughts to drift without control, surveying them with gentle affection, taking mental notes of rare moments that I later transcribed to my notebook as I drank the first pot of tea.

*Sipping the green tea,
my thoughts like rivers flowing,
splash like falling rain.*

With my mind free of noise, I consulted the Book of Changes, patiently manipulating the yarrow stalks in my fingers and only briefly scanning through the interpretations of the hexagrams. The Book of Changes – the I Ching – is one of the oldest surviving texts in the history of literature. In a popular Chinese myth, Confucius is lying on his deathbed. A disciple asks him what he would do if he were given more time on Earth and he replies that he would need at least an extra fifty years to reach an understanding of the I Ching. The book has sixty-four chapters, each represented by a different hexagram. A hexagram is an arrangement of six lines, each of which can either be a yin or a yang, represented by a broken or solid line respectively. The chapters all relate to each other in different ways, so a simple reading from start to finish isn't sufficient for a full understanding. Studied deeply from cover to cover, it serves as a guide to ethical and moral perfection. For some it is used as a tool of divination.

In the afternoons and evenings I played my instrument as Thon had instructed, doing my best to move away from the familiar, avoiding patterns I recognised, striving to generate innovation. Regular consultation with the I Ching helped me to find inspiration and constantly renewed my determination. On one occasion – after perhaps a week or so of isolation – I stumbled upon a staggering passage. I seldom used the text for purposes of prediction, but I was frequently astounded by the relevance of the ancient oracle's response to my dilemmas. Never more so than on this occasion. The hexagram was *Yu* – Enthusiasm or Preparation, composed of two trigrams that represented The Arousing: Thunder and The Receptive: Earth. Each hexagram has an associated passage of text entitled the 'Image'. The Image is an overview, a guide to how the overall text will apply to the given situation. I had consulted the great book with an open question about music; about the changes in my attitude towards it, the chilla, the intuition I had of something elusive and indescribable, the secret potential of blurred and fevered dreams. I wrote down the text.

The Image

Thunder comes resounding out of the earth:
The image of ENTHUSIASM.
Thus the ancient kings made music
In order to honour merit,
And offered it with splendour
To the Supreme Deity,
Inviting their ancestors to be present

I found the following words in the interpretation:

> *From immemorial times the inspiring effect of the invisible sound that moves all hearts and draws them together has mystified mankind. Rulers have made use of this natural taste for music, they elevated it. Music was looked upon as something serious and holy, designed to purify the feelings of men. It fell to music to glorify the virtues of heroes and thus to construct a bridge to the world of the unseen. In the temple, men drew nearer to God with music.*

I was amazed at how precisely my thoughts were reflected in the words. They were telling me that in the wisdom of Ancient China, music was placed in the same sphere as the holy and the spiritual, in the realm of the divine. The sentiments of Lu Bu We echoed through the lines, but this time the source was far more authoritative. I was eager to learn more. For perhaps the first time, I was willing to consider that the I Ching could be employed as a tool of divination.

There was a *changing line*. A changing line in a hexagram yields more detailed information; it reflects shifting trends in any given situation, describing the way circumstances might progress if one makes the right decisions. A line is said to be changing if it is composed fully of either Yin or Yang elements. There was one changing line in the second place of the hexagram: a yin on the cusp of changing to a yang. This was the accompanying text:

> *Firm as a rock. Not a whole day.*
> *Perseverance brings good fortune.*

This describes a person who is not easily misled by illusions. It indicates focus. Confucius made the following comment on the lines:

> *To know the seeds, that is divine indeed. The seeds are the first imperceptible beginning of movement, the first trace of good fortune that shows itself. The superior man perceives the seeds and immediately takes action. He does not even wait a whole day...the superior man knows what is hidden and what is evident.*

I drew back from the pages. Freed of my fingers, they flicked back and forth in the light breeze. Different hexagrams revealed themselves with each gust of air, changing from one to another with a sound like rustling leaves.

I'd never known the book to address music so directly and in such a vivid way, and I was intrigued by the interpretation of the changing lines. I found the page again and re-read the last two lines of Confucius. A new idea gradually came into focus. I looked at my guitar and remembered one of the first dreams I'd written down in my journal. A rush of excitement passed through me like a torrent of icy water. I had to calm myself, relaxing my mind as I did every morning. When my rhythms were gentle, I didn't pick up the instrument as usual. Instead, I concentrated on the sounds of the world, listening attentively to every pulse of nature as it resounded in the vacant spaces of the mountains. I took the stirring of the breeze and the snap and crackle of the undergrowth as instruments, and from the pandemonium of the living world I tried to discern the patterns and melodies of nature's music.

The hours drifted. Night became day, and day became night in a fluid continuum of change. The weather shifted as I listened. The drone of a thousand cicadas ruptured the air; the dry grass rustled; birdsong erupted in furious melodies which died as abruptly as they began. The sun rose and fell with a perfect rhythm, the moon danced counterpoint around the globe. All the while, the earth hummed and juddered with a subsonic tremor. Beneath the percussion of life's movements I discerned a low thrum of unchanging sound. I couldn't stop listening. Did I imagine it? The ear makes its own noises, making it impossible to hear the outside world accurately. As each hour passed, I listened harder, focussing every grain of my being into interpreting the tone. Eventually, I detected that from one direction the hum called with more clarity, moving with an odd flutter like a violin bow in tremulous mid-stutter. I faced it. Dawn was creeping over the horizon, golden rays of sunshine giving warmth to over-cold skin. I was tired, perhaps confused, but my senses were alert. The sound was shadowy and indistinct, but it *was* real.

After some time – I have no idea how many days – I rose from the floor of Doi Inthanon, ate all my remaining food, packed in a flurry of careless activity and mounted my bike. I headed south again, following the noiseless flutter of sound.

I rode wildly over the steaming tar of the road, driven by a sense of urgency. I stopped only when the motorbike between my legs became too hot and rested in the shade to contemplate music or consult the Book of Changes. I seemed to meet people wherever I stopped, but I could not tell which ones were apparitions and which were real. Sometimes they said things that amazed me and I hurtled away with my mind reeling. Towns and villages wrapped around me, smothering my speed, then drifted behind like ghosts as I roared through the night. I was out of time, disjointed from the world.

A young Indian boy told me that the roots of Indian theosophical thought lie wrapped in a mantle of music; that the song lines of the Vedic hymns stand at the very beginning of recorded Hindu mythology. He gave me a copy of the Sama Veda and I learned that Brahma, Shiva and Vishnu were the first musicians. Shiva formulated the infinite modes of rhythm and Brahma and Vishnu accentuated the time beat. I found a picture of Krishna and in his hands he held a flute. He was playing a song to bring back the souls of the people who are lost in maya, a delusional world, the world of our physical, earthly existence. The boy told me he was a 'Bhagavathar'. I asked him what that meant and he told me it was Sanskrit for musician, the literal translation being: 'He who sings the praises of God'. The true masterpieces, he told me, the beautiful few, were all written by devotees to the divine and offered as gifts to the people so they could commune more closely with Atman.

My mind is racing. I must be dreaming now because I am seated on a hard floor and Aristotle is sitting opposite. Instruments fill the room, merging into each other, then separating, their sounds combining into a blur of noise. We are talking about music and he speaks words he has written.

'*It is not easy to determine the nature of music or why anyone should have a knowledge of it*'

A few discordant moments pass between us, then I raise my arms and a flute materialises between my fingers. I blow gently and the instruments find concord and clarity, voicing throes of ecstasy across the room to Aristotle. A thousand notes play in striking and indescribable harmony. His eyes flash crimson as the connection is made. An aurora of pinkish yellow light streams from his belly and mingles with the music in the air. He smiles and says a name that isn't mine. I awake.

But I am still not awake: I'm in a grand hall filled with

obelisks and roughly-hewn rock columns. The ceiling is a sky, the farthest wall is the distant horizon, and the floor is continually shifting. A massive table extends into the distance, filled with exotic foods, bursting fruit and ornate crystal carafes of ruby-red wine. There is music everywhere. It emanates from the mouths of those who dine. I notice Kulitta, the Hittite goddess of music. She sings to Benten, who in turn sings to Euterpe, who sings to Ihy, who sings to Macuilxochitl, who sings to Bes, who sings to Kendatsuba. A circle of melody flies round the room like channelled fire. At the ankles of the gods and goddesses of music, the mischievous Pan plays his pipes. At the head of the table, Apollo sits quietly, listening intently, oceanic eyes flashing glimpses of a world that does not yet exist. He looks into my eyes and I know the melodies before they are sung.

I am riding my motorbike through silence.

After circling the National Park and criss-crossing the central plains, I arrived at the city of Lamphun. I ate in a small cafe and rested in the shade. The afternoon sun was ferocious. The name of the city was familiar. I took out my map, turned it over and found Thon's writing on the back: 'Lamphun'. There was a barely-decipherable road name and the woman's name: 'Nam'.

My conscience was smarting because I hadn't stayed in Doi Inthanon for anything like the forty days Thon had prescribed. I decided to find the woman with a name that meant water. I locked the bike and left my belongings in the safekeeping of the cafe owner, who pointed me in the right direction. A winding back alley faded into disrepair then ruin as the buildings petered out on either side. I found myself stumbling over broken earth, down a dirt track through sprawling rice fields. The dust of a coming harvest filled the air and made me sneeze. I was on the point of giving up when I noticed a solitary hut on the edge of the road. The sun was creeping towards the horizon, and by the time I reached the door the sky was dyeing itself hazy pink. From inside, I heard a noise that reminded me of the flow of sand through fingers, or the trickle of rainwater over a corrugated roof. There were too many notes rolling around each other. I knocked. No answer. Notes fell like water. I knocked again and pushed the door open. The room was small, bare, yet it somehow seemed untidy. There was a sweet fragrance, like ripe mangoes. A woman was bent over a zither-like instrument that spanned a metre or more. An array of frets was placed along a neck that held more than a dozen strings.

I waited for what felt like an hour or more, but it could have been minutes. She seemed oblivious to my presence. Suddenly, without the slightest pause in her playing or change in stance, she looked up. I was trying to decipher the unfamiliar intervals. My face must have shown my confusion because her words addressed my thoughts. Her voice was a monotone, robotic and detached. She told me the oriental tradition of music was more complex than its western counterpart, that it had never developed the 'vertical dimension of chord structure' or the 'dogma of the octave'. Her eyelids fluttered, then closed. I felt somewhat affronted by her words. I hadn't even introduced myself, and she was already denigrating my culture, blurting out her thoughts like a Tourette's sufferer. I tried to ignore her manner, and politely asked about the instrument she was playing. My voice sounded distant and muffled. She answered in the same deadpan tone.

The instrument divided the octave in such a way as to give forty notes as opposed to the twelve that dominate European music. She was in the process of constructing an even more elaborate device that would give eighty notes, resulting in intervals so small that they would be almost impossible to discern. Without thinking, I suggested she try fifty-three notes because the overtones would be more conducive to harmony. She appeared to ignore me, her desert-yellow hair falling across the curve of her dancing right arm as she moved with a flurry into ever-renewing themes and motifs. I stood for several minutes, watching her bare feet tapping the rhythm against the red clay floor. Presuming my audience had come to an end, I moved awkwardly toward the door. As I crossed the threshold she swung her head and spoke again. 'Twelve notes placed arbitrarily upon the continuum of sound? Has the world gone mad? Ha!' She continued to play: arms, legs, hands, body, once more flowing in unison with the instrument and in concordance with the strange sounds. Her eyelids ceased to flutter, and once more I was ignored. Did Thon know what she was like? Perhaps she had changed.

As I stood in the doorway watching the strange figure in swirls of sound, listening to all those unfamiliar notes and exotic intervals, I thought about her words and reluctantly conceded she might have a point. Who had decided how many notes there should be, and why? Sound is a continuous spectrum. It begins below our capacity to hear, runs smoothly to the upper limit of our hearing and continues to higher frequencies beyond our register. A piano has sixty-four keys, but only has twelve notes, repeated as octaves. Between any two points in physical space there exist an infinite number of other points. Theoretically you could keep on halving a distance between them forever, providing you have an infinitely sharp knife. It is the same for the notes on a piano. You could halve the difference in frequency forever if you had an infinitely sharp ear.

I left the hut and stepped into the last rays of the reddening twilight. Feeling nauseous, I staggered and reached out an arm to steady myself on a nearby wall. I was eager to return to the city before dark so as soon as my sickness abated I walked away quickly, listening to the crunch of the dry earth beneath my boots and savouring the lingering aroma of ripe mango that followed me through the rice fields. Lost in my own world, I did not look up until the sound of the dirt road beneath my feet had disappeared and I was back on the tarmac of Lamphun. I recovered my motorbike, thanked the cafe owner and left. I still headed south, but in truth, the reason for that had disappeared – I no longer sensed the fluttering hum.

Sukhothai

I rode as far as I could that day, eventually stopping in the derelict remains of the old city of Sukhothai and pulling the bike on to a patch of loose gravel sheltered by a copse of ancient trees. Hitching the hammock between two of them, I wrapped my blanket around my shoulders and immediately began to fall asleep. As I drifted away, I imagined I saw the gentle spirits of a long-forgotten people rising from the dry earth and floating in the air around me. I had often returned to this place, and although sleeping there was probably illegal, I'd never been caught. Perhaps nobody felt like catching me.

The old pendant engraver is sitting in front of me, dividing the stalks of the I Ching into neat piles. His face has a look of deep concern. I glance at the sticks as they flick nimbly through his fingers. His movements are agitated. Is he questioning the response before he's completed the reading? He knows he should return the book to its place on the highest shelf, but he cannot stop. I'm worried.

His archaic instruments are blurring in and out of the shadows around him. They're all moving and making noise, all playing the same single note. Except one, which plays a harsh note that repeats with a grating urgency. I try to trace the source of the aberration, but I can't tell where it's coming from. The engraver appears to hear it too. He is clearly unsettled.

I move closer. I call out. He doesn't respond. He doesn't appear to see me. His fingers count out the sticks in a series of convulsive motions. Am I here? Can he see me? Reaching out, I lift his face towards mine. He looks me straight in the eye without recognition. The dissonance grows harsher and scratches at my inner ear, which begins to ache. The engraver's eyes are like water trapped beneath a thin layer of ice. I stare into their consuming, translucent depths, mesmerised. Suddenly his features fade, blurring as if melting. His face disappears, giving way to a fluid metal mask. I recoil, transfixed, apprehensive. The stalks snap in his hands. The muscles in his fingers shake with tension. His whole body becomes rigid, and when I look back at the place where his face should be, I see my own eyes staring out. I stare back and the image twists in on itself, collapsing back into shimmering molten metal.

I hear a soft sound. It emanates from the fluid. It's a reflection, my reflection. I am mere sound: ephemeral, formless, and free. A set of concentric circles materialises, as if a stone has been cast into the glistening pond and the subsequent ripples flash-frozen. It stays there for a few seconds then falls apart. Another shape appears: more complex, more symmetrical. Then it too subsides into chaos and a thousand shapes come and go in a cascading flurry that I struggle to keep up with. Eventually, only one shape remains. There's a bright light in the centre. Three other lights surround it, connected by a circle. It rotates very slowly, pulsating with the rhythm of a heartbeat, emitting the soft hum that I recognise as my reflection. For a moment everything is still, but it doesn't last. The mirror suddenly explodes, hurling a barrage of sonic waves through the air, battering my skin, invading each and every one of my internal organs and shaking them inside me. I feel dissonance like a violent cramp in every limb. It is my dissonance, my unresolved tension. It is my reflection. The other instruments are hiding in the shadows, their voices silenced by fear. There's nowhere for me to go. I brace myself against the onslaught and wait it out.

The world is absolutely silent. I am surrounded by utter blackness. The engraver's face appears. It is a mirror once more. My pendant comes into focus. It pulsates and bends under an unknown pressure. Like all of the other shapes I have seen, the strain eventually overwhelms it. It breaks asunder in a spray of harmless, tiny grains and I awake.

The darkness was thick and heavy. The moon was high but hidden in clouds. The sounds of the distant jungle were barely audible. My breathing was rapid and tight, my heart was pounding in my chest. I was in shock, traumatised by the intensity of the dream. When I looked around, the only shapes I could discern were the creeping finger-like shadows of the branches of the trees. I was suffocating in darkness. My hand reached instinctively to my heart and I realised something was missing. There was no cord around my neck; the pendant was gone! Shock magnified into panic. I rolled out of my hammock and scrambled on all fours, shining my torch into every crevice, casting rocks aside and brushing away the gravel, but it was futile. *Where could it be? Did it fall from the bike? It could be anywhere. Is it in the mountains of Doi Inthanon? On the road? Which road? Where did I lose it? In the cafe? Where did it fall?*

Then I remembered the words: *Has the world gone mad?* Nam! I remembered the reddening twilight on a hard clay floor, and suddenly recalled hearing the faint noise of something hitting that floor.

Within minutes, I was back on the bike. I rode away from the ruins and on to the main road. The rice plains peeled away behind me, a lone rider in the timeless night with icy wind blowing holes in my skin. I rode north until the first tentacles of dawn broke the black of the night.

The bamboo hut was deserted. My pendant was lying on the ground outside, broken in two. A mangy cat was pawing it idly in the muddy heat of the morning sun. As I approached, it limped into the shadows, keeping half an eye on me. I picked up the pendant and held it in my clenched fist for a few moments, gazing at the empty fields and the sprawl of rice paddies. Everything was so still, so quiet. The smell of ripe mangoes had disappeared and without the colourful backdrop of a setting sun the whole atmosphere had changed. I wondered where the woman had gone and how she had left so quickly, without leaving the slightest trace of her presence. Perhaps she was hiding with the pendant engraver? I unfurled my fingers to reveal the broken halves of the pendant with the familiar script of the engraver delicately etched into the sides: *Where there is pure music there can be no evil.* I never spoke to him about the phrasing of the inscription. The sentiment was familiar, but its validity was tenuous.

In Russia, the serial music of Webern and Schoenberg was banned for being conducive to social disorder. In Maoist China, Beethoven's Fidelio was banned for supposedly encouraging individual freedoms. In the Middle Ages, a single interval was banned by the Catholic Church because it identified with the Devil: the tritone, *musica in diabolus*. The harmony of the spheres was held to be a manifestation of God's love, and the tritone was a stain on the perfection of His bounty, the musical representation of original sin itself. It was of the Devil. If you played this interval, you not only invoked the Fallen Angel – you took him inside you. Music has been misused often in the past, warped and trivialised for base aims and misguided plots, corrupted and obscured by fanatical motives.

To truly appreciate music you must let it dance alone...

Perhaps the engraver etched his symbols on to my pendant with these thoughts in mind. Perhaps the crux of his message lay in the use of the word 'pure', and the distinction to be made between 'music' and 'pure music'? Perhaps his message was an invocation to discernment, to a sense of the ideal that somehow differentiates between the mere playing of instruments and another kind of music?

I was standing outside Nam's abandoned hut. The sun was now higher and I held a broken pendant in my hand. I noticed a tiny chamber concealed within the ivory, so I blew into the hollow and shook the thing violently, but nothing fell out. Why had the engraver given me this particular pendant — because it was hollow? If so, why was it empty? Flinging the pieces of the pendant aside, I fell on to my knees and began searching the ground. In my mind I saw the phoenix, the flame and the warm and welcoming sound of pipes in a distant dream. I cleared away stone after stone until the area was bare earth, flat and clean. After an hour or so of searching, I found a delicately-folded piece of silk-thin paper covered in dusty earth. The sun was rising and the first direct rays were warming my face. I blew the dirt away and opened it to reveal a place name which I was surprised to find I recognised. It was in Northern Laos, near China. Although I had never been there, I had come close during my travels. There was also a tiny map, drawn with remarkable skill, still intact and readable. It showed a track into the jungle, at the end of which there was what looked like a collection of huts, a village perhaps. In the bottom left hand corner there was a small triangle of dots. The only other information was one word in English script that I didn't understand: 'lus'.

I placed the paper in my wallet and sat beneath the leaves of a bamboo. It was clear the engraver had hidden this deliberately. I had to act upon it, just as I had gone to Doi Inthanon at the behest of Thon. I had nothing else to do, nowhere else to go. I was deeply curious. But for the time being, I needed to sit and just let nothing happen. I was exhausted. I pined for a soft bed, a duvet and endless cups of tea, but it was pointless to think about such things. The peaceful isolation of the empty hut was good enough. I set the alarm to wake me a few hours later and slept.

Fire. White-hot light. A phoenix appears. It gathers its wings, swells to bursting and changes explosively. As feathers fly from its body in jets of flame, I see, in the ashes, tubes of luminescent wood. Air blows through them and the sound they make is pure and warm. I close my eyes. The noise comforts me, and as I listen, I feel as though I am floating viscerally among the long-dead spirits of the ruined city of Sukhothai. Somewhere in the background, someone is watching. I sense he is waiting, but for what, I have no idea. I seek him out, but every room I enter is identical to the one I leave. The stairs and corridors all lead onto themselves in bewildering and impossible complexity. I cannot find him. I run. Nothing changes, but I run anyway. I run until exhaustion wakes me.

I pulled out the map of South-East Asia and found the area in Laos where the village in the engraver's map should have been. It wasn't marked. I rubbed the bleariness of sleep from my eyes but I still could not see it. The area was high in the northern hills between Phongsali and the Chinese border and the village appeared to be near to the town of Hat Xa. The journey would take me up the Nam Tha River, through stunning scenery of uninterrupted jungle. I took heart, straddled the bike, kicked the starter and headed for Chiang Mai, intending to rest in a real bed and visit Thon. The road sped beneath me and in no time at all I was entering the bustling chaos of Chiang Mai's busy streets. Horns beeped incessantly on the canal road, motorbikes cut in and out of traffic like furious ants, cars hustled each other, their fumes mingling with the smell of bad meat and frying noodles. The vibrancy of the atmosphere sent a surge of adrenalin through my weary body. I rode in circles, staking a claim for lanes I had no reason to be in, speeding past trucks, cutting in needlessly, and roaring away from traffic lights as they changed. Eventually I drifted into the back alleys of the eastern quarter, slowing my pace to a more appropriate crawl. Thon's home came into view. It had only been a few weeks since I had last seen him, and he would presumably expect me to be in Doi Inthanon, diligently exhausting myself with my guitar and the I Ching. I was apprehensive: how would he react when I returned after only two weeks? I had managed to get lost on my bike for a few days and visit Lamphun, which left not much more than a week of diligence under my belt. But I knew where I was going next, which brought me some comfort.

I pulled up outside the house and the purr of the motorbike died in a random click of contracting metal. The familiar sounds of Thon's guitar rose above the harsh clatter of the city. I knocked gently, and entered quietly. He was deep in concentration. I sat down close to the door without saying a word. Our eyes met briefly, but his were focussed on other things and mine were slowly closing. He turned his attention back to his guitar. I lit a cigarette, lay down and listened to the reflections of his music on the corrugated walls. I slept.

When I awoke all was quiet and Thon was hunched over the stove attending to the preparation of tea. I sat and watched the tender and precise movements, sensing the air of calm that accompanied every action, taking care not to distract him until he was finished. After perhaps five minutes, he turned to me, handed me a cup with a smile and spoke for the first time since my arrival.

'Sawai-dee Krap, my friend.'

'Sawai-dee Krap, Thon. It is good to see you.'

'It is good to see you my friend. You are very tired, and you have arrived early, but that is okay.'

I started to explain, but he stopped me. We spent most of the afternoon playing music and talking about inconsequential things. It was exactly what I needed: rest and relaxation. I spent several days with him, sharing most of the details of my two weeks. He didn't make any comments or judgements about the brevity of my chilla, which surprised me. He seemed to have changed since our last meeting, which I found a little disconcerting. He was more withdrawn, as if distracted. I didn't take this personally, because he seemed pleased to see me, but he was distant at times. It made me realise that I didn't really know much about him. I had spent nearly three months in his company, but even after a close companionship with someone, an unexpected revelation can easily rock the foundations of your familiarity. What did I really know of Thon? In truth, very little. At times I thought the study of music might be the cause of his distraction. He seemed much more focussed and relaxed when he was playing his instruments, but it certainly served to encourage his distant moods. His illness had abated and he was less prone to coughing fits. This might have been attributed to the greater frequency and intensity of his playing. The music he played now had an ethereal quality that was not there two weeks before. He had stopped playing in the bars and cafes altogether. This alarmed me, because it was his only source of income as far as I was aware.

After a few days, I began to feel restless. I took out the engraver's map as we drank tea around the fire. Thon had barely spoken all day, but he livened up and took interest, and I was keen to take advantage of his loquacious mood. I finished the story of my recent travels and finally told him everything that had happened before I first met him: the engraver, the pendant, and how I found the map. He knew the place, he knew the man – he didn't say so, but I could tell from the change in his demeanour. He was excited, and the change was palpable. He told me I should go at once. Unlike the time before, I was in complete agreement.

'What about Nam? Did you find her?'

I explained the visit in detail, and he looked both concerned and amused at the same time. I told him my true feelings, which essentially boiled down to the fact that I thought she was a little unhinged. At the same time I had to admit that when we'd met my nerves had been frayed. I asked him if he knew where she might have gone in such a hurry, suggesting that her destination might be a favourite haunt of pendant engravers. He laughed and reiterated his opinion that I should go to Laos.

'I've made up my mind to do it,' I said, 'I'll find the village and see what happens, but to be honest, I'm confused by everything that's happened since I arrived here.'

He looked serious for a moment, then his face broadened into a mischievous smile. The flippant delivery of what followed was a contrast to the remoteness I had grown accustomed to over the last few days. He grinned as if all my old friends were lying in wait behind a doorway and were about to leap out and celebrate my birthday. 'Go north, Sebastian! Seek out this man and enjoy looking for what you don't know you're looking for. You are like a pinball let loose on the world, my friend, a pinball bouncing around in my beautiful country.' And he chuckled some more. It was lovely to see him so unrestrained and carefree, and I laughed with him happily. When his merriment died away he told me I should leave in the morning. He returned to his music, leaving me to pack my things and visit a few of my old haunts in the city. I had a sneaking suspicion that Thon had been to the village in the hills of Laos. Early the next morning I packed my things, collected my visa, said my farewells and set off.

I arrived in Chiang Rai within hours. A local mechanic agreed to store my motorbike, and I made for the border town of Chiang Khong by bus. Touching the edge of Thailand by early afternoon, I headed straight to the jetty, crossed the Mekong and returned to Laos.

Thon's words rang true: I did feel like a pinball bouncing around his country. But I was glad to be back in Laos, I'd always found the pace of life there more laid-back and easygoing than Thailand, typified by an old folk saying that a Laotian farmer had once recounted to me. I'd asked him why he never ventured into the nearby city of Luang Prabang: *I have my rice, I have my cooker, I have my family – I am happy.* When the developed world came to his land to introduce the benefits of modern farming techniques, they were dumbfound by the collision of ideas: *'Why work for a whole year to accumulate 'wealth' when I can work for six months and spend the other half of the year sitting on my porch, sipping rice wine, playing with my children or just enjoying the world?'*

I booked into a cheap guesthouse and began networking with tourist groups to find company for the passage up the Nam Tha, eventually gathering enough people to charter a slowboat. We were due to leave the next morning for the three-day trip north. I was pleased to be moving so quickly. The rivers were high and it was perfect weather. My travelling companions came from all corners of the world, most of them seeking adventure and excitement before returning to a future of climbing career ladders and trying to buy houses they couldn't afford. Presumably I would one day follow them. I joined them for a while as they sampled the destructive forces of *lao-lao* whisky, smoked cheap weed and shared stories about the road. It was good to sit down, relax and listen to their tales so I stayed up for a while, but my energy flagged before theirs and I was the first to leave.

    I got up as soon as my eyes were open, knocked on all the doors, shuffled the hung-over travellers through their breakfasts, down the street and into the boat where the pilot was waiting. Ten minutes later the engine roared into life, rattling our bones as we forged a path through the thick gravy sludge of the Mekong. The sound drowned out conversation and we passed along the mighty river with only our own thoughts for company, sliding through chocolate-brown waters surrounded by deep jungle greens and cloudy blue skies. Several hours later, we left the Mekong and headed north into the Nam Tha tributary. China lay directly ahead, and between that great nation and our little boat, a small village that was not marked on the map was waiting for me. All I had to do was find it.

Phongsali

As we powered up the river on the final day of the trip, the jungle became less dense, the water became muddy once more and by early afternoon we entered the shallow scum of the city river system.

I barely paid attention to Luang Nam Tha when we arrived. I'd been there before and it was a nondescript city full of dust. I went into the first hotel I encountered to arrange transport to Phongsali and Hat Xa and found I was in luck: an overnight truck was leaving in two hours. I paid, and sat outside by the roadside to wait. The wheels of rattling motorbikes raised dust on the wide road. All kinds of people passed by, going about their business, paying me no heed. I lit a cigarette and put it out. I lit another and put that one out. I'd just given up smoking.

We travelled through rolling hills and fire-cleared forest, clattering through the serenity of late-night Laos in our battered old truck, crashing through the silence. The northern hills were like ghostly sentries silhouetted against the sky. I was standing in the back of the truck, holding the roof-rack with one hand and leaning against the back-rails to avoid falling out. My arms were aching. Inside, the truck was packed with hill-tribe people and their animals, tradesmen with their wares and a few travellers discovering the bounce and bungle of Laos-style truck-transport for the first time. Most of them tried to sleep, their heads rocking with the erratic movement. I tried to relax and absorb the jolts by staring upwards into the void or playing music in my mind – simple music, calm music. I closed my eyes and recalled an old man with a pendant, the vast plateaus of Tibet, a sign that swayed on a stage, a jungle in a dream, a phoenix, a triangle of dots, a pattern of lights, guitars, pianos, numbers, colours, squares, circles, wheels...

At 2 am, we entered the thick mists of Phongsali. A blanket of white hung over everything and blurred the world into vague, imaginary shapes. On the winding mountain road that led up to this eerie place – broken and torn with rippling scars of clay – visibility was near zero. To the left, I could make out steeply banked slopes of heavy dipterocarp, to the right an abyss covered by delicate veils of mist and punctuated by random upthrusts of the forest canopy. Giant fernlike trees were juxtaposed with the skeletal corpses of once-great species, lining the horizon and lending the scene the ominous aspect of a disused, ancient graveyard. It made me tremble with expectation. When we arrived, the city itself was invisible and had to be navigated by touch alone. I found a room, fell asleep, and began to dream, although the whole journey in the truck had seemed like a dream.

I am standing at the edge of an overgrown forest. The foliage is dense, dark and forbidding and I'm trying to find a gap, the slightest hint of a way in. There is none. Wherever I look, the foliage is denser, as if the muscles of the forest are contracting. The darkness follows wherever I go. I turn my back in despair and see an endless desert. The shadows of trees stretch away, their tips touching the horizon. The trees never move despite the breeze that ripples through the canopy.

I turn again to the forest, swinging my gaze back and forth: the blank sky, the desert, back to the forest. The trees are creaking and groaning. I hear every sound and focus on each one with my eyes closed. A light forms behind my eyelids, a reddening where once there was darkness. At first I see dots. They form a pattern, one, two, three, then four. I open my eyes and a shaft of brilliant yellow light comes through the forest and strikes the earth just in front of me. It forms a shape in the sand: a circle at the centre, then smooth-cornered triangles in precession, then another blurry circle. I place my hand on the pattern of light. A wisp of dry sand rises around my palm. The light ascends with it, shining in my face. I lower my head and raise my hand to my forehead. As I turn my palm outward, I find I can guide the beam wherever I choose. Rising from the floor with my arm outstretched, I follow a path that materialises around the ray of light. Eventually I reach a grove of bamboo. In the centre I see a man who holds his right hand towards me. The light is coming from his hand. It strikes my palm and returns to him. The air is humming with a complex, yet soothing, vibration. I lower my hand and the light strikes me in the eyes, overloading my mind with thoughts. I fall to my knees and am suddenly awake.

I got out of bed, packed my things, paid my bill, shouldered my rucksack and left. It was still early and the world was filled with mist and fog. Trudging happily over the tarmac, I studied the tiny map from the pendant. The path I wanted was on the other side of Hat Xa, but it looked as though I could avoid passing through the town by leaving the main road earlier and crossing some open fields. By the time I left the road, it was late afternoon. The fog had dissipated and the air was clear and refreshing. My limbs still ached, reminders of the horrendous journey to Phongsali the day before. I crossed the fields without incident and found the path easily, crossing rivers and elephant trails, evading the writhing, ravenous leeches and trying in vain to answer the call of distant monkeys.

Several hours later, I found myself in a bamboo grove where several simple huts stood. The only sound came from the forest. The sky was beginning to darken. A young woman dressed in a simple robe was treading silently from hut to hut, lighting lamps. When she saw me, she beckoned. As I moved closer, I saw eyes like an ocean, soft skin, animal grace. She introduced herself as 'Kun' and led me to one of the huts. Inside, there was a simple wooden bed with blankets, a desk with objects arranged neatly upon it and a small fire that glowed and crackled. She ushered me to the bed and told me in a soft voice to lie down and sleep. I was exhausted from the strenuous walk, the restless night in Phongsali and the rigorous truck journey the day before. I followed her bidding without protest and was instantly asleep, deeply and peacefully. I had arrived.

Part 2 – Musica Humana

The soul of music slumbers in the shell
Till waked and kindled by the master's spell;
And feeling hearts, touch them but rightly, pour
A thousand melodies unheard of before

Samuel Rogers

Kun/Ch'ien

The village was small, six or seven huts straddling a narrow, fast-moving river. Dense woodland rose sharply on each side, concealing the valley from the rest of the world and hiding the stars. It should have been a dark and claustrophobic place, but it wasn't. The river ran east to west, providing a corridor through which the light of the sun travelled. Sunrise was magical. Pinks and reds danced along the river and faded into yellow as morning broke, flooding the water with radiance. During the day the floor of the valley was bathed in dappled golden light, as entrancing and beautiful as a flickering flame. Nothing stops moving, not for an instant.

    I had been there for over a week without meeting the man I had come to see. It did not concern me, I was happy and relaxed. Kun had taken it upon herself to look after me during the week, taking me on meandering jungle walks, to nearby waterfalls and into enchanted caves where rivers ran like whispers through the darkness. We took lanterns into the depths of the mountain, talked softly about different worlds and scratched tiny pictures onto the walls. The light from the lanterns gave them life and we watched them dancing with the shadows. Under clear night skies we listened to the sounds of the natural world rustling through the forest around us, sitting in silence for hours. She was warm and sincere, vibrant, gentle, unerring in her enthusiasm for life, peaceful and thoughtful, kind and beautiful. Her presence was so distracting I often forgot why I had come to the village.

I tentatively brought up the purpose of my visit, asking her who I had come to meet. It seemed an odd question to ask, but the only clue I had was the symbol on the tiny sheet of silk-thin paper, which I showed her. His name was Ch'ien, she told me, but he was away. At first that was all she would say. At least I knew that he existed and I was in the right place, albeit at the wrong time. Later, she told me he was visiting friends in China and would return soon. I had no desire to leave.

On the seventh or eighth day of my stay we sat together on a rock by the river. The sun was slipping out of the western sky, burning red holes through the jungle canopy. Kun was playing her Chinese flute. I was listening quietly, bathing my feet in the cool crystal water, absorbing the gentle patterns of sound and turning them into fantastic tales: her melody was the voice of an ancient spirit lost in an unfamiliar and endlessly shifting landscape. The river called with mellifluous gurgles and splashes, but the spirit couldn't hear it and ran on and on through the quickly-moving shadows, neither gaining nor losing ground. The sadness of the river was unbearable. It wept inconsolably. Its tears became glistening drops of harmony. The shadows clung to them and became still. The landscape became less chaotic and the spirit heard the river's voice. It swam down the river until it reached the sea, where it was swallowed into the depths, into the huge well of tears that springs forth from the middle of the earth, a place of quiet rage where everything is fashioned from bricks of fire and flame.

She finished the piece and we both sat in silence. The

river carried the melody away and washed the images out of my mind. As Kun could not be drawn on the subject of Ch'ien, I took the opportunity to ask her about the *lus*. She asked me why I wanted to know. I produced the map again and showed her the tiny word in the bottom right corner.

'What are these?' She pointed at the triangle of dots in the bottom left.

'I've no idea. The same symbol was on the engraver's door, though they disappeared when he did.' I'd already told her the story of the engraver. 'I've seen it somewhere else as well, but I can't remember where.'

'I've seen it too, I think.'

We stared, trying in vain to recollect where we had seen the pattern of dots. She broke the silence by returning to my original question.

'It is unusual for me to speak about such things with people who have come to see Ch'ien.'

'Why?'

'He is a teacher, and I am a student.'

'Did he teach you about the *lus*, whatever it is?'

'Yes.'

'Will he teach me?'

'I don't know. He will decide when he meets you.'

'Can't you tell me anything?'

I'd travelled a long way to get to this village and I still had no idea why I was there.

'Ch'ien will probably explain fully when he returns, but I can tell you something about them.' She stood up, brushing the dust from her robe. 'Come, we shall return to the village. Stories are best enjoyed over tea.'

The water boiled slowly, the fire burned bright and the tea was sweeter than usual. We were alone. Kun straightened her back and began.

'At the dawn of musical time, the Yellow Emperor sent Ling Lun, known as the "Music Master" into the wilderness of the western provinces of China. His mission was to search the vast forests for a unique shoot of bamboo, which when blown would produce a foundation tone for the dynasty. If he failed – if he took the wrong note back to the Emperor – it was said rains would fail, disease would strike and famine and hardship would drive the peasants to revolt. The dynasty would collapse in disharmony. The tone was seen as a sacred eternal principle, an absolute pitch, sometimes referred to as a man's voice speaking without passion, more often as the call of a rare bird honoured by the ancients for its divine spirit. The note that Ling Lun found was called the *huang chung*, or "yellow bell". The *huang chung* was important. They even used the pipe as their standard measure of weight and length, keeping it locked away in the *Yueh fu* – the government Ministry of Music.'

In the ensuing pause, I should have asked how the Music Master knew when he had the right note, and how the Emperor knew when it was laid before him. What if they had disagreed? But Kun continued before I had a chance to speak. 'In one of the ancient texts called the *Yueh Chi* – The Memorial of Music – it says that *music expresses the accord of heaven and earth*. Perhaps the person who gave you the pendant spoke of these things?'

'No, he didn't.'

'Well, the *huang chung* was the foundation upon which this accord was built. It was used as a template, as a starting point for a set of pipes called the "*lus* pipes". The procedure for making the pipes comes from another of the five classics of ancient Chinese literature, the I Ching. Do you know how the numerology of the I Ching works?'

'I know a little, but please, tell me everything.'

'To build a hexagram, you use the sticks to produce three numbers, which added together determine the nature of each line, yin or yang. This is where the numerology comes in. The numeral 1 represents everything that lies beyond the capacity of the human mind to comprehend: the ineffable, Tao, God, or whatever word you wish to use to plug the gaps. The choice of word is a personal one, but the 'ridgepole' is used to describe it to students – a simple line. If you have a line, then you automatically have two sides of it. The universe is filled with lines, be they the tiniest grains of matter or the most advanced of human ideas. The fabric of the world is a balance of dual forces, of energy and matter. The interchange between these two fundamental opposites across the line of the Tao is what gives rise to the world we live in. In your culture…'

'e equals mc squared…'

'Exactly, but instead of the Tao, you have the constant speed of light, around which energy and matter continually interchange. In your culture, the Tao has been replaced by c, the speed of revelation.'

'But energy and matter are not like yin and yang. They're scientific terms.'

'A great deal is known about the properties and behaviours of energy and matter, but very little is known about *what they actually are*. The tiniest grains of the stuff are elusive. They escape the lenses of the most powerful microscopes. They are not as far removed from yin and yang as you might think.'

'So the numeral 2 represents the world of duality, the physical world, the universe we see around us?'

'And feel with our bodies, and hear and smell and taste – the substantial world. The realm of the spirit, of heaven, was given the numeral 3. So 1 represents the Tao, 2 the physical earth and 3 the heavens. The yarrow stalks deal with the physical and the heavenly when they are forming the hexagram'

'And how does this tie into music?'

'Patience Sebastian, I'm telling you a story. The Music Master consulted the I Ching before and during his search for the *huang chung*. He used it to give him directions as he travelled through the wilderness. The hexagrams guided him to the node of bamboo. The bamboo was crafted into the *huang chung* pipe, and its note, regardless of the pitch, served as a middle C for the entire dynasty. This is how intimately the I Ching is woven into the culture of Chinese music.

'When the Music Master returned to the palace of the Yellow Emperor, a second pipe was made. It was exactly two-thirds the length of the original. Another pipe was then constructed, which was exactly four-thirds the length of the second pipe. The process was repeated in alternation – two-thirds then four-thirds then two-thirds then four-thirds – until twelve pipes were made. These were called the lus pipes.'

'Why two-thirds and four-thirds?'

'In the Record of Rites, it says: *since three is the numeral of heaven and two that of the earth, sounds in the ratio two to three harmonise as heaven and earth.* The pipes were made using the ratio of two-thirds, and four-thirds. In this way, the music of the pipes should accord with heaven and earth.'

'And you get a scale of twelve notes, like we have in Europe?'

'Not quite. We do get twelve notes, but we don't use them as a scale. Remember that the twelve notes are produced for a very specific reason: music expresses the accord of heaven and earth. There are twelve months in the year, twelve hours in a day and twelve hours in the night. These are the natural cycles of heaven and earth. The twelve notes give twelve different musical keys, one for each of the months and each of the hours. In this way it was believed that a musician could play the music that most accords with the rhythms and melodies of the natural world at any given time.'

'Music was played in a different key with each passing month?'

'And with each hour. Chinese music has scales with five notes: *kung, shang, chiao, chih* and *yu*. These are perhaps like your doh, re, me, fah, sol. The root note, *kung*, is always taken from one of the twelve *lus* pipes and the other four higher notes of the scale are found in the same way as before: two thirds then four thirds then two thirds then four thirds.'

'So instead of having a twelve note scale, you have twelve different scales, each one used for a different time of the day, month and year?'

'Exactly. And the Emperors took it very seriously. The Chinese 'Book of History' says that Emperors in the third millennium took odes of the court and ballads of the village to see if they corresponded with the five notes. They had to be sure that everyone was playing the right notes. The well-being of the dynasty depended on it.'

'It's complicated.'

'Even more than you might think. In the astrological charts, one complete cycle takes sixty years. The twelve different animals of the zodiac each appear five times per cycle, so there are five sub cycles. Music in the third year of the Fire Snake would be different to the music in the first, second, fourth and fifth years of the same zodiac sign. Certain melodic tendencies would rise to prominence in each year, and wouldn't repeat for another sixty years. Most of this has been forgotten for a long time, but...'

'I see that Kun is looking after you well.' I spun around and saw a monk in a flowing gown. I recognised his face from somewhere – a dream? He stood above me with a benevolent smile as Kun introduced us, then he spoke again. 'I am glad that you have arrived, Sebastian. I began to worry as time passed and you did not appear, but all is well now. I am sorry I was not here when you arrived, and also that I am very tired and I have to sleep. We will speak later. If you need anything, I'm sure Kun will continue to help you.' He left as silently as he had arrived, disappearing into a hut at the far end of the village. Kun took the kettle from the fire, washed out the cups, said goodnight and followed Ch'ien. I was stunned. I realised I hadn't said a word to the man I had travelled so far to meet. I went to my hut and played my guitar quietly, unable to sleep with thoughts of what the next day might bring. The story of the *lus* pipes filled my mind.

I awoke at five next morning with a shadow across my face: Ch'ien's. The sounds of the jungle hovered in the air, a teapot steamed on the table next to two delicate porcelain teacups and two banana-leaf wraps of sweet rice and coconut. Breakfast.

'The morning has arrived, Sebastian. You have slept well. How do you feel?'

'Good, thank you,' I replied, squinting and rubbing my eyes. Ch'ien sat down as the morning sun entered the hut.

'We shall eat, drink tea and talk.' He handed me the rice and poured tea. I sat on my bed eating the rice with my fingers. 'Sebastian, do you know why you are here?'

'Have I come to learn about the *lus* pipes?'

'You have not, Sebastian. Though your answer is close.'

I felt he was enjoying my silent confusion in a mischievous way. 'You have come here to make your own *lus* pipes.

Kun has already told you about the traditional *lus* pipes, and what an important role they have played in history.' He took a mouthful of rice, then a sip of tea. He seemed fond of dramatic pauses. 'Think of a dynasty as being a smaller part of something much bigger – the planet, or even better, the whole universe. Think of a human as being a smaller part of a dynasty. All three exist simultaneously as parts of the same thing, but all three can also be treated as individual machines. To understand the dynasty, the ruler must learn the ways of both man and the universe, the individual and the unified, the great and the small...'

'The yin and the yang.'

'Yes. Could it be possible to look at the soul of a man and recognise that it looks exactly the same as the entire universe, but on a much smaller scale? It's simply a matter of where and what you are, and what eyes you use... But you may be asking what this has to do with you, Sebastian?'

I said nothing. I'd once looked down a powerful microscope at a plate of copper and was struck by its appearance. It looked uncannily like an aerial photograph of a mountain landscape. I thought I knew what he meant.

'You will construct the *lus* pipes while you are here. Just as the dynasties of the past constructed their pipes according to the spirit of their times and their nature, so will you. While you are here, you will find your *tone*, your yellow bell, from which all other notes derive. Think of it as finding your own musical key, your natural pitch. I will help you as I am able, but success is ultimately in your own hands. I'm sure you'll do well. Do you have any questions?'

I couldn't think of a single one. My mind was blank, but I felt I should say something. I was going to find and fashion my own *lus* pipes. The thought had never crossed my mind. I suddenly remembered a dream. It provided me with a question: 'This may sound strange, Ch'ien, but before I came here I had a dream. I saw a pendant, my pendant. It blew apart, and I saw a shining phoenix that went on to became a set of golden pipes. There was a stranger in the dream, but I couldn't see him. I knew he was present, but not who he was or why he was there. I think the pipes were the *lus* pipes, because there were twelve of them tied together. But why was there a phoenix in my dream? And who was the stranger – you?'

'Who gave you the pendant?'

I told him about the engraver and the map that guided me to his village. He asked me what I thought had prompted the engraver to give me the second pendant. I realised it was the poem and recited it to Ch'ien.

'The words you spoke are not yours alone.'

'What?'

'*I'd find the perfect rhythm, the golden cosmic note – the one they made in heaven, the one the angels wrote; for it had a golden note.* – I wrote the same lines myself over forty years ago. Before I wrote them, others had too. Many people have had the pleasure of waking up with those words in their minds. I wouldn't let it worry you. The phoenix you spoke of is the phoenix of the *p'ai hsiao*. It is a traditional way of arranging the *lus* pipes with the six yin pipes and six yang pipes spiralling outward in opposing directions. It represents the phoenix with its wings closed around itself. Do you have a copy of the I Ching?'

'Yes.'

'Then I suggest you spend today in preparation, and leave for the jungle tomorrow. To begin with, head west. Consult the book whenever you feel doubtful or unsure. Pack some food, but be prepared to find your own food and water – it's not too difficult in a forest like this. I must go now, I have many things to do. If you need me I will be in one of the huts. One final thing: to the best of my knowledge I don't have a habit of appearing in other people's dreams. Your stranger must be someone else.'

I sat alone with my half-eaten breakfast and mulled over his words: the poem was not mine alone? He too had written the words and so had others? So where were they coming from, and why did I hear them? Beethoven stepped into my thoughts again:

> *You ask me where I get my ideas. They come unsummoned, directly, indirectly – I could seize them with my hands – out in the open air, in the woods, while walking, in the silence of the nights, at dawn, excited by moods which are translated by the poet into words and by me into tones that sound and roar and storm about me till I have set them down in notes. They come unbidden.*

Songs always arrive unbidden, but the gentle caress of the muse is recognisable. I can say with absolute certainty that it was absent when the poem came to me. Perhaps the mysterious dream stranger put them there. I occasionally felt a similar presence when I was awake, though I may have been remembering dreams. When that happened, I sensed someone else in the room, intimately close, as if we were holding hands. *The superior man knows what is hidden and what is evident*, the I Ching had said. What hope was there for me?

The superior man perceives the seeds and immediately takes action. He does not even wait a whole day...

I packed my things and headed into the jungle.

Huang Chung

As soon as I was clear of the village and enclosed by the jungle, I sat down on the moist earth and unfolded the silk sheet to reveal the I Ching. Noting the position of the sun, I turned to face south, laid the sheet on the floor, placed the book on top of it to my left, and lit an incense cone. The yarrow stalks were tied in a bundle with a strap of old leather. I untied them and held the sticks between my hands, rolling them forward and back, listening to the soft clicking sounds and allowing the cleansing aromas of the incense to pass over the dry wood. Selecting one from the pile, I placed it directly in front of me on the dark blue silk. The stick, chosen at random, represents the ridgepole, the dividing line around which the yin and the yang forever cycle and transmute. Once everything was arranged, I held the remaining forty-nine sticks in one hand, placed my other hand on the I Ching, took several deep breaths and tried to visualise the object I was seeking. Somewhere amongst the countless million shoots and leaves of the jungle, there was a node of bamboo with my name on it. I tried to see it in my mind. I imagined a small grove of bamboo, light pouring from the skies, vivid green foliage, leafcutters scurrying through the undergrowth, drops of water clinging to branches and the echoing calls of distant monkeys. I imagined the smell of the earth, muddy and fresh, the warmth of the sun on my skin and the wetness of the forest air. In my imagination, I saw a cluster of bamboo stalks. At first they all looked the same, but then I saw one that was different from all the others. It drew my full attention. I held its shape in my mind, opened my eyes and began to cast the I Ching, dividing the forty-nine sticks into piles, determining each line of the hexagram slowly and with care. The result was very clear. The hexagram was composed of two identical trigrams – Tui, which represents the West. The Judgement of the hexagram was: *The joyous; Success; Perseverance is favourable.*

I wandered in a consistently westerly direction. Each morning I focussed my thoughts on the innocuous bamboo, then manipulated the stalks and read the corresponding chapter of the I Ching. Sometimes I veered north, other times a little way south, but I always maintained a westerly course. Perhaps I crossed the border and entered China, I had no way of knowing.

I'd taken packets of rice, cured meat, dried fish, and a bag of fruit. I also had two flasks of water, some sugar and a large bag of salt. Kun had insisted I take this to keep the leeches away. I soon ran out of water, but I was able to gather rainwater or drink from streams and springs. When I ran out of food I ate what I could find: fruit, tiny fishes and insects that tasted like salty popcorn. Kun had given me a crash course on how to survive. Though eating insects had initially disturbed me, I soon realised how valuable they were as a source of nutrition. Hunger was always close, but I managed to find enough food to keep me going. Nights were challenging. When darkness fell, the immediacy and the sheer volume of the jungle enthralled and terrified me. Insects clicked and rasped at the air, trees and leaves came alive with rustling menace, distant rivers hissed. The occasional unidentifiable noise awoke in me a stifling sensation of danger. I slept restlessly on the ground, surrounded by a thin line of salt, my senses always alert. I tried to construct makeshift shelters, but soon realised that they weren't worth the time and effort. I hung my possessions from the treetops, risking a possible invasion by monkeys rather than the certainty of an invasion by bugs. The insects were the worst: I could not tell by their appearance how hard they could bite, or with what venom.

More than a week passed before I came within reach of my goal. I had cast the I Ching first thing in the morning and followed its directions as usual, heading slightly south, but still maintaining a generally westerly route. The Image of the hexagram reflected a state of completion, of resolution. I tried not to think too hard about it in case I was misinterpreting the words, but I was very careful to stay alert and watchful as I walked on. At noon I found myself in a sparse clearing of bamboo. Sunlight streamed through the opening and imbued the jungle floor with a golden hue. I lay down and rested in the warm rays, my eyes closed and my arms spread out. I tried to visualise the node of bamboo with my name on it, and there it was at the very front of my mind, hovering in the air, its edges cleanly cut, its sides clean and smooth. I tried to hold it in my mind, opened my eyes and looked around. Hundreds of shoots reached up from the dark earth. I could see them all, but none appeared unique, and I felt nothing extraordinary as I surveyed them. I repeated the process, conjuring up the ideal node in my mind and quickly opening my eyes to stare out at the world and find a connection. It didn't work. I cut one of the smaller trees regardless, carefully removing a single node. I filed the ends and made a hole at the top, turning it into a pipe – the *huang chung*. It looked okay. The sides were smooth, the edges were cleanly cut and it was straight. I raised it to my lips, gathered in my breath and blew loudly across the aperture. The noise was neither smooth nor clean. If anything, it warbled and was slightly harsh. Throwing it aside I cut another one, filing it carefully and cutting the hole as before. The tone was muddy and flat. I spent half an hour in this manner: cutting, blowing and hurling and getting nowhere. Finally I gave up, dropped the knife and sat upon the forest floor. Deep down, I knew that I could not walk any further into the jungle. I had reached the limit of my endurance and I wanted to go back to the village.

I imagined my arrival. Kun would embrace me and we'd talk excitedly about my adventure. A fine meal would be prepared and we would drink rice wine and warm coconut milk by the fire. The moon would be full, our bodies would be warm and the air would carry the aromas of cinnamon and toast. Ch'ien would arrive in his flowing robes, interrupting Kun's flute-playing to ask me where my pipes were. I would confess that I had given up my search due to fatigue, hunger, and a lack of will. He would look at me with disappointment, my head would drop and Kun would look away.

I didn't know what to do. The last words Ch'ien had said drifted in and out of my consciousness but I could glean nothing from them. I had already gone over everything he had said on the morning I left, and I was certain I had not missed anything significant. Perhaps I was being too hard on myself, over-thinking? It might be okay to get up, walk until it felt like a good time to stop, bend over and reach out for the nearest piece of bamboo. But it would be wrong. Something told me that Ch'ien would know if I had taken a short cut. I closed my eyes, stopped thinking and opted for a few moments of emptiness. Cicadas droned, monkeys called to one another in the distant treetops and the forest floor rustled. I knew the sounds well and could immediately sense any change, any intrusive element. I noticed such a change now, a flapping sound that fluttered through the air with increasing volume and clarity. The sound of beating wings.

I sat up and opened my eyes as the noise stopped. As I did so, the bird took flight again in a commotion of feathers a few metres from where I lay. I watched it as a child watches an escaped balloon spiralling into the endless atmosphere, following as it rose higher and higher, shrinking with every turn until it eventually disappeared from view. A single crimson and gold feather remained. I reached out, and found my hand resting on a shaft of bamboo. As if waking from a dream, I regained my senses and reached for the knife with a single-minded focus. I cut the node, filed the ends, made the groove, held it to my mouth and blew. The sound filled the jungle. It was clear and powerful, resonant, bright, smooth with the warmth of deep undertones. The note continued to echo through the jungle after I ceased to blow, passing from tree to tree, causing the leaves to shiver, the insects to raise their mandibles, the monkeys to cast their eyes in my direction, curious and wondering. On it went, until the jungle smothered it, absorbing the vibrations in its leaves and ligaments. For moments I stood immobile beside the strong arms of the bamboo. I could still sense the sound rippling over the ground somewhere in the distance, too quiet to be heard. I returned to the tree from which I had taken the node and hurriedly cut down a dozen or so more, gathered them in a bundle and wrapped them in my blanket. I would need them to complete the *p'ai-hsiao*. Wasting no time, I left the bamboo grove and headed back.

The journey was easier because I was more familiar with the jungle. I knew my direction and how long it would take, a certainty that bolstered my will and drove me to walk with more determination. I slept little and rarely stopped to rest or find food. I became an automated walking machine, following the sun in the morning and turning my back on it as evening came. Everyday at twilight, I lifted my nose and sharpened my ears, hoping to smell the smoke of the fire or catch a fluttering flute note that would guide me home. I drew comfort from the fact that if I overshot the village, I'd inevitably hit the road to Hat Xa and could retrace my steps. As long as I kept going east, I couldn't get lost. I reached the village in five days, arriving just after dark. It was quiet and nobody was around. I went to my hut and collapsed, exhausted, on my bed.

I had plenty of time for contemplation while walking back to the village. I recalled Thon's stories about his friend Nathalia, and was struck by the similarities between the ancient Tibetan traditions and the Chinese. Although the two neighbouring nations are now effectively one, they were separate in their early development. The high cultures of ancient China developed on the eastern fringes of the continent, well removed from the plateaus of Tibet. Yet both cultures developed independent theories of music that sought to bridge the gap between the corporeal and ethereal worlds of form and spirit. What were the words that Confucius had said?

> *It fell to music to...construct a bridge to the world of the unseen. In the temple, men drew near to God with music.*

And in Tibet they did the same, pursuing the mysterious yogic chords with instruments of wood and bone. All cultures use music to invoke joy, and most of them employ it to invoke trance-like states or experiences of unified communion. But do they all have this historic tradition of striving to perfect the language of music in order to constantly improve understanding of the ethereal world where the spirit dwells?

Is this held as an enduring purpose of music everywhere? Stravinsky thought so:

The profound meaning of music and its essential aim... is to promote a communion, a union of man with his fellow man and with the Supreme Being.

When Handel wrote his Messiah in a twenty-four day mania, he erupted from his solitude, exclaiming:

I saw all of heaven before me, and the Great God himself!

Was this the venting of an entirely understandable delirium, or a reliable description of a genuine experience?

Or Brahms:

I felt that I was in tune with the infinite... there is no thrill like it.

Schumann heard: 'music that is so glorious, and with instruments sounding more wonderful than one ever hears on the earth' while he slept. Entire symphonies were sung to him by what he referred to as angels. In the morning, when he was unable to translate the beauty of their voices onto the stave, they turned into devils and tortured him. By the end of his life, the ultimate form of musical self-harm took hold: the final chord of his final composition stayed in his mind always, preventing him from composing anything new and giving him no peace. Silence is an essential nutrient for every musician. He committed suicide.

Did all of these people suffer from the lunacy so often lauded as a bedfellow of genius? Were they all passing comment on mere delusion, or were they providing evidence of the kind of experiences described by the yogi of Tibet and the ancient sages of China? I had no idea what lay at the root of my own musical heritage. How did Europeans find music, and what was written in our ancient texts?

When I awoke Kun was sitting over me with a damp cloth. On the bedside table there was a tray of food, a jug of water and some fruit. Incense was burning and the smoke was dancing in the light of the sun. As my eyes took this in, she dabbed my forehead with the cloth and said something I didn't quite catch. I was amazed how soft the pillow was, and the mattress. Without saying anything, I reached under the bed and pulled out the bundle of bamboo. She unwrapped it and I picked out the *huang chung* and passed it to her. Holding it in her delicate hands, she nodded her approval with a smile and took a piece of silk out of her pocket, wrapped it around the bamboo and placed it on the bedside table. I tried to eat but was too tired. She kissed me on the forehead and left. I fell back into sleep almost immediately.

Several hours later, I rose and devoured the food. The room was empty. I stretched every muscle, yawned deeply, gathered the bundle and the pipe and headed for one of the huts which was used as a workshop. Ch'ien was there, deep in concentration, playing a zither. I quietly emptied the contents of the bundle onto one of the benches and began inspecting the bamboo, looking for the most suitable with which to fashion the first of the eleven pipes that would complete the *p'ai hsiao*. Ch'ien continued to play behind me as I gently chiselled and filed in time with his melody.

Three or four hours later, we began to talk. He was excited by my return and demanded to know everything that had happened. I gave him all the details: embarrassing anecdotes about finding food and fighting the onslaught of bugs, the intricacies of the final few moments before I found the *huang chung*, including the reasons I had known I had found the right node. He watched me closely. We talked into the night, sitting by the fire with endless cups of tea and the occasional rice wine. Kun was nowhere to be seen.

For the next few days I worked at the *p'ai hsiao* for four or five hours each day. Ch'ien would often sit with me and play his zither or make repairs to his other instruments. I was under no pressure to finish quickly. He reprimanded me several times for working too fast and not paying enough attention and encouraged me to slow down at every opportunity.

In the mornings I went for walks through the forest with Kun, trekking up the stream and stopping to play music with the trickling of the cascading water. We usually talked about discussions I'd had with Ch'ien. She was always willing to listen. At the time I thought she enjoyed our conversations, but in retrospect she may not have. I sensed a sadness in her that I couldn't understand and made no attempt to unravel. I was preoccupied with making the *p'ai hsiao*, with my thoughts, with myself. Perhaps it was inevitable. At midday I would meditate for an hour before taking lunch and heading to the workshop. I carefully perfected the *huang chung*, smoothing the edges and decorating and polishing the shaft. I constructed the other eleven pipes in the manner prescribed by Kun and Ch'ien. As each one was completed I blew through them consecutively to ensure the correct notes were being produced. As I blew down the ninth pipe, shortly after two o'clock on the fourth day, I felt Ch'ien's arm on my shoulder.

'Come Sebastian. You have worked hard these past few days. Go and collect your guitar. We shall spend the afternoon playing music together.' He reached across the table and lifted the *huang chung* from the table, rolling it in his hands and inspecting the craftsmanship. Leaving him to his inspection, I headed towards my room. I washed my hands, changed my clothes, tuned the guitar and wandered over to Ch'ien's hut. Kun was still in the workshop. I could see the silhouette of her body crouched over the smelting pot, preparing the fires for action.

Ch'ien sat across the fire from me with his zither across his lap, a pot of tea to one side and a tray of his own hand-rolled banana-leaf cigarettes on the other. He introduced me to the zither, showing me how it was made and telling me how the strings were related to each other. Though the *p'ai hsiao* pipes were revered as being symbolic of man's accord with nature, the zither was without doubt the preferred instrument of the ancient philosophers. In Chinese the instrument is called the Ch'in, which means: 'to prohibit; to check the evil passions, rectify the heart and guide the actions of the body'. Seven strings lie flat above a fretless soundboard and are tuned to the Chinese pentatonic scale. You play it by pressing the string on to the board in one of thirteen positions, each marked with a strip of ivory. Construction of the instrument is an incredibly demanding and precise undertaking, embodying a vast system of cosmological philosophy. An equally vast array of symbols was introduced in order to describe the numerous subtleties of technique – there were twenty-six specific types of vibrato alone. The zither is the instrument you see in the hands of Confucius in the ancient reliefs. He used it as a means of meditation, a source of inspiration and a path to spiritual understanding.

I retuned my guitar several times to find the sweetest concord with his instrument and we played together, laughing at our mistakes and losing ourselves in our successes. It was very relaxed and easy. A few hours later, Kun came to the door with a package wrapped in silk. She placed it to one side of Ch'ien and left without speaking a word. The atmosphere changed immediately. Our frivolous mood was transformed in an instant to one of earnest gravity. Ch'ien returned the zither to its case and locked it. He returned to his seat and sat for a moment before he spoke.

'Your time with us is coming to an end Sebastian. There is something I want you to see before you go. It may not be easy, so you'll have to trust me. Do you?'

'Yes.'

'Then take the package that Kun gave you and follow me.'

'Okay.'

I took the package and followed him. It was heavy and hollow on one side, like a bowl. I trusted Ch'ien implicitly, but his prologue had made me nervous. As we walked away, I saw Kun in the workshop, staring into the fire, lips pursed and brow tense.

We left the village, scrambling up a steep, rocky incline through thick vegetation. There was no path. The jungle was moving slowly into night, the moon and the sun throwing a wan yellow light on to the canopy. Ch'ien pressed on ahead, a ghostly silhouette gliding along a path I could barely see. After an hour or so, we emerged into a clearing. A granite face towered above us. At its base there was a cave entrance, black and full of menace. Ch'ien took a candle from under a slate, lit it and passed it to me.

'If you follow the passage that leads from this first cave, Sebastian, you will eventually reach a small, egg-shaped chamber deep within the mountain. To get to it you will have to squeeze through narrow fissures. They will become even narrower as you proceed, but do not fear. Do not turn back. When you get to the space, you will find a cross etched into the floor. Next to this there will be a box of matches. Take the package you hold in your hands – it is a prayer bowl – and sit on the cross. Place the bowl before you and extinguish the candle. Leave it next to the matches. Do you understand, Sebastian? It is important. It must be done correctly.'

'I do.'

'Good. Next, do the following: focus for a single hour on the noise around you, the sounds of the cave, the groaning of the earth, the dripping of water. Chase all other thoughts from your head, Sebastian, and try not to lose your concentration. After one hour, pick up the bowl, stretch out your arms and make it sing. Then focus on its voice.' Ch'ien stopped and peered at me. His eyes were as white as bone, but the pupils were flickering in the light of the torch. I nodded that I had understood, and he continued. 'This is the difficult part, Sebastian: do not stop until I come to fetch you. I will guard the entrance. Nothing will follow you in. You will be safe. Do you understand?'

My mind was confused. I understood the instructions, but not the reason I had to follow them. I nodded, held out the candle to the crevice of rock and tried to see into the blackness. Without another word, Ch'ien ushered me forward, his hand at my back, and I began my descent into the belly of the mountain. With each successive step, the granite walls crept closer and the air seemed to grow thinner and colder. Ch'ien took his hand away and the mountain engulfed me.

For half an hour or more I walked on, over dribbling water, past gleaming walls of metallic stone that flickered in the half light of the candle flame, step by step downwards into what I imagined to be the underworld. The ceiling and floor gradually closed in and I was forced to crawl, desperately trying to keep the flame alight. I began to feel entombed. A flush of panic paralysed me. What was I doing? This was sheer lunacy. Was Ch'ien playing some hideous trick? Was

Kun involved? I remembered the look on her face as she stared into the dancing flames. Of course she knew where I was. I could feel her with me.

'Do you trust me Sebastian?'

A voice in my head replied 'yes', and I knew I couldn't turn back. I gathered my strength and pushed onwards, all the while suspecting that the world had gone mad, and me with it. Minutes later, I emerged with a twist of my hips into a perfect egg-shaped chamber. Heaving in a deep breath, I was grateful for some space and the ability to once again stand erect. The flame flickered as its light filled the silent spaces with a yellow glow. Shivers ran up and down my spine. This was the cave. It felt oddly familiar.

The Cave

In the dim glimmer of flame, I see the cross carved in the floor, and close by, the matchbox. I sit down, unwrap the bowl and beater, lay the silk on the ground in front of me and place them on it. Everything is arranged, but I am nervous. I flatten the silk, turn the bowl, check the matchbox again, then look around. The walls are perfectly smooth, unnaturally so. The only blemish I can see is the tiny opening through which I entered. Way above, through convolutions of torn and twisted rock, Ch'ien is keeping vigil at the mouth of the cave. The flame draws in air from his direction. It ties me to the world.

I take several deep breaths, steel myself against fear and blow the candle out. Blackness engulfs me, utter blackness. Adrenaline soars through my veins, my heart races. It is all I can hear, pounding like a blacksmith's hammer against the invisible stone walls. I close my eyes. Nothing changes. Gradually, my heartbeat slows. The adrenalin drains from my system. My gasping breath softens. I calm myself with focussed meditation: breathing, not thinking, breathing... breathing, not thinking, breathing...

Water is dripping in the distance. There's a faint hum coming from all directions. I can't tell if my ears are playing tricks or it's the sound of the earth gripping itself together. I am mesmerised, and I listen more intently, straining my ears to make them work harder and with more precision. The depth of concentration slows me further: breathing, not thinking, breathing...

I fell through layers of consciousness, peeling back the veils and drifting into empty space. The humming of the earth gave way to a kind of static, like the crackling white noise of an out-of-tune radio. I forgot that I was sitting in a cave in the heart of a strange mountain. I forgot that I was supported by my legs and that my arms hung limp at my sides, that the action of my lungs caused air to be drawn into my body, and that the distant pulsing of my heart was fuelling my brain with blood and oxygen. I lost track of time. Had I been there an hour? Had it been two, or three, or barely a half?

I lift the prayer bowl from the floor and stretch out my arms. A delicate noise breaks the silence when I tap the edge, followed by a whining drone that accumulates volume as I circle the wooden beater around the rim. I can discern different notes playing, beating softly against one another. When I feel them tickling inside me, I understand the cave. It's perfectly ovoid, and I am seated at one of the focal points. With my arms outstretched, I'm holding the bowl at the other focal point. The sound made by the bowl reflects from the walls and is replicated at the focus within my body. I can feel the vibration inside me like fingers stroked through hair. I almost stop tracing the circles in surprise, but my arms continue to move, and the music continues. It's louder now. I can't hear anything else. I open my eyes, but there is only sound, saturating everything, filling every space, congealing into walls of rock, dripping from the ceiling, hanging in the air and seeping through the floor. If I were to move, I'd be swimming. Breathing, not thinking, breathing...breathing, not thinking...

The beats disappear. I can only hear one note. It's entrancing. My mind hums and burns. All the while, time is passing, drifting through the air like flowing water. I am flowing too.

Silence. Was I sleeping? I can think again, but remember no transition. I can't see the world.

I'm in the cave. The sound permeates everything, but I've heard it for so long and so deeply that my mind must be operating around it. I've been sitting here for hours. It might be days. I can no longer feel the motion of my arm circling the beater around the prayer bowl. I can no longer feel my limbs. The sound is there, ringing, reverberating, encircling my body and mind. I can feel it moving inside me again.

My heart leaps, and freezes in mid-beat. The pressure of the world strikes. Something else is in the room, but everything has petrified, nothing moves. Time ceases completely; not a single thing happens.

Silence and stillness, like a gap torn in time.

I rise from the floor with legs like jelly. Friendly hands help me. A warm body presses against mine. My arms hang at my sides, my knees ache and my ankles are numb. I am unbearably cold, trembling violently, and hungry too. My skin is full of pins. A voice? Ch'ien. He's helping me leave the cave. He's easing me out between the narrow walls. He's speaking but I can't hear.

I opened my eyes and saw Kun. I had the strangest thought: Ch'ien sends me to near-death experiences and Kun brings me back, a neat arrangement. She smiled down and asked how I felt. I moved my legs and arms, stretched my toes and clenched my fists, drew in a deep breath that turned into a yawn, and gave myself a clean bill of health. I was at peace. In fact, it felt like any other morning that might follow a very deep and peaceful sleep. I had a raging appetite, which Kun had anticipated. Once more, a feast was waiting on the bedside table. Before I touched the food, I drank all the water, but was still thirsty. Kun left to refill the jug. I finished every scrap of food. When the newly-filled jug appeared, Ch'ien was carrying it. I drained its contents.

Ch'ien came straight to the point: 'Well, Sebastian, what did you find in the cave?'

I lay back. Ch'ien sat quietly with his eyes upon me. Many thoughts went through my head. I couldn't give him an easy answer. 'I was hoping you might be able to tell me.'

'I wasn't there, Sebastian.' He wasn't going to give me any help.

'I think I found a kind of musical silence. No...wait...I have to think.'

'Tell me what you heard as you played the bowl. Tell me about the changes.'

I sat up. 'Okay. I struck the rim with the beater and sounded the bowl. At first I heard different notes, a blend of overtones, gently harmonising, all pulling towards a kind of centre. The intervals got smaller, but there was no dissonance, the whole process was soothing. Then they merged together into one note, but all the other notes were still there...does that make sense?'

'If that's how it felt. What then?'

'It merged, wrapped into itself...difficult to explain... It felt as if I was wrapped in it too. And everything else: the walls, the air, the water, the blackness. I was engulfed. It was still cold, but I'd stopped feeling it. I'd stopped feeling *me*, my arms, my legs. If I could feel anything, it was the note, but I could feel it here, Ch'ien.' I thumped my chest. Ch'ien said nothing. 'It must have returned several times because often I would notice it again, as if I'd been reawoken by it. I have no memory, I wasn't conscious, I had no awareness. I wasn't there.'

Ch'ien waited patiently.

'It was beautiful, Ch'ien. At times it was relaxing, calming, confusing, but above all, beautiful.'

'Yes.' He leaned back and exhaled the word slowly. With one hand, he tugged at his beard. With his other, he tapped a rhythm on the chair arm. His brow was furrowed.

'What was it, Chi'en?'

His eyes met mine. I held his gaze as the tension filled the space between us. He leaned towards me again. 'What you found in the cave is a kind of music that nobody else will ever hear. Not me, not Kun, not Thon, none of your friends or family, or anyone. It is yours alone, the voice of your own soul, singing.' He leaned back, seemingly waiting for my reaction. I stared at him and stayed silent. 'Kun and I crafted your prayer bowl. We made it after you returned from the jungle with the *huang chung*.'

I still said nothing. A prickly heat rose on my skin.

'A well-crafted prayer bowl sings with seven separate notes. When the bowl warms up, and when you circle the rim with the correct speed and pressure, the notes can appear to coalesce. The bowl is designed to resonate with the same note as your own *huang chung*. The shifting states of your soul were in perfect resonance with the note from the bowl, and so, from your perspective they became undetectable.'

'My soul?'

'That which endures.'

My mind raced, my skin was itchy and moist. I saw flashes, tiny specks of light in the air. I closed my eyes and I could still see them I felt pressure against my forehead, sat up in bed and a bolt of lightning coursed across my back. Goose bumps rose and the hairs on my neck bristled. My chest was numb. 'I know this, Ch'ien' My voice sounded strange, as if I had left it in the cave and it was echoing from there.

'You know *what*, Sebastian?'

'I know what you're talking about, I know. It's *musica humana*, the second class of music – the music of the soul: that which endures. I have heard of it, I know of it. But it's just a myth.'

'What are you saying, Sebastian?'

'It's a myth; it's not true.'

'What isn't true? Tell me what you're talking about!'

'For every *Republic* there's a library of junk.'

'What?'

'Thales thought the world was water; Anaximenes thought it was air; Diogenes lived in a barrel, for God's sake. Madness and delusion! But Pythagoras believed in the music of the spheres.' My skin seethed and my head was filled with white-hot metal. I pressed my hands against my temples.

'Wait! I have to think... I must talk... He said there were three forms of music in all. *Musica instrumentalis* is the music we make on guitars and pianos, and on pipes. The second, *musica humana*, fetters the body to the mind, gluing them together with the stuff of the soul, a continuous but unheard vibration of thoughts, feelings, senses, the harmonic resonance of body and soul. Our lives, no, our spirits, are like melodies. We screen it out because it's always there, but it exists. It can be heard. 'Pythagoras heard it in others. He used instruments to induce resonance, to alter the states of their soul, to coax them into different keys and change their rhythm. The soul can overpower the body. That's how he healed, using the natural laws of harmony and dissonance. The soul is moved by music. This is where it began, this is how it started. Plato regulated the use of the modes – moods? You see, they're from the same word.'

'And the third?'

'The third is *musica mundana* – the music of the spheres. More mysterious, more difficult to describe. In the beginning there was the word, and the word was… But what would it mean to understand this form, to hear *musica mundana*? You must start with the first, progress to the second, master the second, then approach the third. You have to be careful. You have to be thorough. You have to begin…'

'Sebastian!'

It felt as if my body was wrapped in cling film. I was drenched in sweat and gasping for breath.

'Breathe deeply. Take your time.'

'I don't know what's happening. Where is this coming from? What am I talking about, Ch'ien? I must be repeating the pages of books I've read. But how could I forget? How could I know it? What happened in the cave?' For the first time since I'd started talking, I looked at Ch'ien closely. His face was ashen, his skin drawn and his eyes narrow and fixed. I felt weak and ill. I was confused. I was saying things I didn't understand and I had an overwhelming feeling that they were not entirely my own. A question came to mind, which was definitely my own.

'Ch'ien.'

'Yes.'

'How long was I in the cave?'

'Three days. You slept for another two.'

I fell back on my pillow as if I had been punched in the stomach. I had just spent three days without food or water, sitting on my own in a tiny cave listening to a single note of music. Had I been circling the beater around the bowl for three days? Impossible. Three days in the damp and cold heart of a mountain, thousand of miles away from my home. Two days asleep. That made five days in total. I felt faint.

Ch'ien called for Kun. When she arrived he asked her, in a whisper, to make some tea. I lay on the bed, staring directly ahead, unblinking, unthinking. My skin was crawling with shivers. I was in shock.

'Do you remember much about this man Pythagoras?'

Talking was still easier than thinking.

'I know a little. He was born on Samos, an island on the Persian coast. I need a drink.'

Ch'ien poured me a generous glass and passed it to me. The words rasped in my throat as I spoke. Every breath I took felt like a drag on a mouthful of cheap cigarettes. I took a swallow and carried on.

'He was different from the others, mysterious in his day. People said he was superhuman, capable of incredible feats of reason, of miracles. Some said it was magic. He taught reincarnation, claiming proof of the transubstantiation of the soul. Did he actually claim that? I can't remember. Nobody else did, at least as far as I know. He went to Italy when the Persian armies came and built a school there. He taught people to invoke the higher levels of Harmony. He taught them how to heal with it. He was looking for *musica mundana*.'

'And did he find it?'

'I don't know? Perhaps he did. His teachings were secret. I don't think anyone knows, except for him. But I imagine he's very much dead by now... My head hurts.'

'You should rest for a while. I will leave you.'

'Ch'ien, I want to go back.'

'What?'

'The cave. I want to go back.'

We sat in silence for a while, looking at each other.

'Not right now obviously, but sometime.'

'Rest, Sebastian. We'll talk again later.'

As he said those final words, I thought he looked old, old

and weary. Had the wrinkles of age etched deeper into the folds of his skin in the last five days? He was visibly shaken. I was so tired and my head ached. Perhaps I was imagining the changes. My skin felt sharp and tender from shivering and my throat was dry and painful. Where were those words from? *Musica humana, musica mundana?* I'd never heard of them until the moment they came from my mouth. Pythagoras was a scholar and a mathematician, a philosopher who discovered the hypotenuse and left a legacy of tedious geometric equations for me to learn at school. Who was this occult figure with miraculous powers I had just described to Ch'ien? What the hell happened in the cave, *musica humana?* I had to go back, but Ch'ien's reticence suggested he would probably forbid it. Too many thoughts and too much confusion. I fell asleep for another two days.

A Triangle of Dots

It was early morning and the birds were still silent. A candle flickered next to my bed. The walls of the hut glowed orange, the shadows quivering as the candle-flame danced in a draught from the door. I thought about turning over and getting more sleep, but I was wide awake. How long had I slept? I had no idea, but I felt refreshed. The pain in my head had gone and my body had stopped sending distress signals. I sat up and poured a cup of water from the flask on the table next to the bed. After three cupfuls, I sipped more slowly and began to think more clearly. Out of habit, I flicked open my dream journal and searched my memory, but all I could find was an image of Ch'ien leaving my room, his head lowered and his feet dragging on the floor. And the cave.

Taking the journal with me, I left the hut and ventured outdoors.

It is dawn. Sun is streaming through the trees. A plume of smoke rises from the smouldering ashes of the evening fire, lazily entwining the cold air. A monkey cries out for its breakfast, cicadas hum quietly, birds wake and sing. A deep breath of the crisp air nearly knocks me over. I've wandered through the village, over the stream, to the edge of the forest, circling the bamboo grove, turning back, going nowhere and enjoying every-

where. I feel docile, a domestic animal secretly coiled like a wild one. I'm enjoying the simple pleasure of being, feeling the air, watching the light on the water, breathing, not thinking, breathing, not thinking.

Kun emerged from her hut looking radiant. She didn't notice me sitting by the edge of the forest as she went about her business, rekindling the ashes, collecting water from the stream, tidying and sweeping the dirt from the fire. I watched her, admiring her delicate beauty: her limbs like the swaying branches of a willow, her steps effortless. Every morning she carried out the same tasks. Normally she and Ch'ien were alone in this hideaway in the forest. I relished my existence, spending my days searching out ever-greater depths of beauty: in her, and the world around.

I was about to write my thoughts down, but she lifted her head and our eyes met before the pen struck the page.

'You're awake! How do you feel?'

'I feel wonderful. How are you, Kun?'

'Well.'

'How long did I sleep?'

'Two days. We were worried.' A wry smile curled her lips into a familiar arc, but something about this conversation was unnatural.

'I might as well have been dead for two days, I slept so deeply. But I feel much better.' I took a seat by the fire and rinsed out the clay teacups as the kettle began to steam. Kun continued to sweep, and for the first time since my arrival, we shared an uncomfortable silence. 'I think I'll be leaving soon, Kun.'

'I know.'

The clunk of clay on clay, the sweep and whoosh of the brush, the crackle of the fire, the click and whistle of the forest, Kun's feet shuffling.

'Where will you go?'

'I'm not sure. Perhaps go and see Thon for a while.'

'Ch'ien speaks of leaving also.'

'Ch'ien! Where is he going?'

'I don't know. He's been here for years, but now he speaks of leaving.'

'He's not coming back?'

'It sounds like it.'

The kettle had boiled during the last two sentences, screeching insistently through our words. I wrapped a cloth around my hand, reached across and lifted it off the fire. Kun continued to sweep, although there was no ash on the floor, and no leaves.

'When you came out of that cave four days ago, something changed. I don't know what happened, and it is not my business to ask, but something has changed in Ch'ien. He is tired.'

'Why would he want to leave?'

'I don't know. I was going to ask you the same question. All I can do is wait and see what happens.'

'What will you do? If he goes?'

The sound of her brush was beginning to grate.

'Go with him.'

Her answer didn't surprise me. I had no idea what kind of relationship she had with Ch'ien, but realised they were tied to each other by bonds I did not understand. Part of me was sad, part angry. I'd only known her a few weeks, I didn't know her well at all. I arranged the cups on the wooden table. Kun sat down and started preparing the tea.

'Kun.'

'Yes.'

'Did Thon come here?'

'I think so... many years ago. Before I arrived.'
'Did he go into the cave?'
'I believe he did.'
'What happened?'
'I don't know. As I said, I was not here, and it is not my business to ask. My understanding is that Ch'ien and he became close. He comes here occasionally. Ch'ien probably visits him when he travels. Why?'
'No reason. Just wondering.'
She passed me a cup of tea.
'Have *you* been in the cave?'
'Yes.'
'And?'
'And what?'
'What happened?'
'It's not your business to ask, Sebastian.'

Ch'ien didn't join us for breakfast. I drank tea with Kun then returned to the workshop to finish the pipes. I still had three more to construct. It took me most of the day, and when I finally finished, I felt sad. I wanted to leave, to spend time alone and try to make sense of what had happened. I wanted to see Thon. I assembled the pipes in the phoenix configuration of my dream then sought out Ch'ien. He was deep in meditation in one of the huts, sitting on a cushion on the floor with a lazy half-smile on his lips, eyelids flickering. I sat down outside and patiently waited for his reflections to come to an end. I sat for an hour and still Ch'ien hadn't moved. I meditated by the door of the hut, laying the pipes to the side and focusing my thoughts on the sound I had heard in the cave. I could almost sense the vibrations, but they were memories. I chased them, trying to manifest the sensations by a sheer force of will, but it was hopeless.

An arm fell on my shoulder, pulling me gently back to the world. I opened my eyes and saw the familiar figure of Ch'ien. He was smiling. His eyes were smiling.

'I hear you are leaving, Sebastian.'

'I think so, Ch'ien. I hear you are too?'

'I'm going away for a few days, but I'll return. Where will you go?'

'I'm not sure.'

'To Thon?'

'I think so, but I'll take my time. I've no idea where I will go afterwards.'

'I wouldn't worry too much; you will find your way.' He paused, then continued, 'I have a gift for you before you go.'

He led me to a hut and we sat down. He handed me a package wrapped in silk. I unwrapped it and recognised the prayer bowl and beater. I held them up. It was the first time I'd seen the instrument that had orchestrated the strange experience of the cave: simple, undecorated but obviously well-crafted. There was another small package. I lifted it out.

'Open that later,' he said.

'Okay. Thank you, Ch'ien.'

'You're welcome. Keep it with you always and you shall not want for friends.'

'Will you do me a favour?'

'If it is in my power to do so.'

'Will you look after my pipes? The rigours of travel would only ruin them, and I have the bowl now. It would mean a lot if I knew they were in safe hands. I could maybe return sometime in the future to fetch them.'

'Of course.'

I passed him the *p'ai hsiao*: twelve pipes curled around in the phoenix formation of six yin and six yang pipes. Ch'ien rolled them in his hands and studied the craftsmanship before nodding his approval and offering me a smile of respectful pride. I could see why Kun was uneasy. Ch'ien had changed. He was not the same man who had ushered me into the cave several days ago. His body language spoke of resignation. He'd aged in appearance. I'd never thought of him as old but now he looked ancient. I was worried and confused.

'Kun is worried,' I said. 'She doesn't understand what is happening.'

'And you?'

'I have ideas.'

'I have been here for more years than I can remember. Many people have searched me out. Before me, there was another, and before her, another. There is a great tradition and purpose to this place. I would like Kun to join the tradition when I pass away, but we shall have to wait and see what happens. It may be time for the jungle to reclaim it, or perhaps, our work here may be just beginning. Sebastian, you have your own path to walk. When you go, go in peace, and we will both share that peace. In the meantime, you could treat me to a performance on your pipes. Will you?'

'Of course, though I'll be making it up as I go along. I haven't played them yet.'

'It's often the best way, and at least they're well-tuned, eh?' He smiled and said, 'I have a favour to ask. I have a note for Thon. Will you take it?'

'Of course.'

'I will be leaving early in the morning, so please take it now. Then we shall say our goodbyes after the concert has finished.'

The next morning I gathered my belongings and made ready to leave. Ch'ien had already left. Kun was ill at ease, but she hid her emotions as she wished me luck. She filled my bottle with iced tea and gave me dried meats and packets of coconut rice, wrapping them neatly in cloth and placing them in my bag while I was clearing up the hut. I watched her fingers as they worked – such grace!

I gave her a final embrace, then turned towards the jungle and left. Very soon I left the village behind. The sounds of the jungle grew louder. I was alone, moving again.

After a mile or so, the path widened out to a dirt track – just as I'd remembered. I was about to veer off the road and head through the forest when I heard a noise, a faint rumbling. I stood and listened as it drew nearer, then a glint of reflected sunlight caught my eye. Over the brow of the hill, far down the track, I saw a vehicle heading in my direction. It was a white Landrover, which could only be heading for Ch'ien's bamboo grove. I considered waiting to find out who was coming. Perhaps it was Thon? Or Ch'ien returning to tell me something he'd forgotten to say before he left? I ducked into the foliage. It was unlikely that Thon would travel so far unless his health had significantly improved, and Ch'ien was not forgetful. Besides, the distraction of the Landrover guaranteed privacy for what I planned to do next.

I walked back in the direction of the village, then veered into the jungle. A few minutes later, I heard the Landrover pass a hundred yards to my left. It stopped, no doubt because the track had become too narrow. I carried on, navigating by intuition, alert for any recognisable landmarks. I saw none, but eventually stumbled into a shaded clearing. The rock face hid the sun, and at its foot, the mouth of the cave was gaping. I stood and listened. What did I expect to hear? Ch'ien had left the village long before I had awoken and must be miles away by now. Kun had no reason to be here, and besides, she'd probably be talking with whoever was in the Landrover. I went to the base of the cliff, took a candle from beneath the slate, hid my bag under a bush and walked into the cave entrance. The sunlight fell away and the air immediately grew colder. I lit the candle, and with the prayer bowl in my other hand, I headed down.

As I entered the inner cave, I was surprised and disappointed by how ordinary it seemed. Perhaps I had expected the air to be charged some kind of magical quality? But it was simply a hollow in a mountain. I sat down on the cross with the prayer bowl in front of me and the matches beside me. I took a few deep breaths before I blew out the candle. Silence fell with the darkness and engulfed me. My first thought was of Ch'ien. He wasn't waiting for me this time. He wasn't keeping a vigil at the mouth of the cave. His arm wouldn't materialise on my shoulder. No-one would help me back to the surface. I was alone. But I was unafraid. The human body is a dark cave too. I began to meditate, focusing intently on the barely audible whispering. A calm encircled my mind. First I heard the static, like a rainstorm on gentle waters, as I had last time. The white noise subsided as my ears homed in on the ambient hum. Time began to drag and freeze. I reached for the bowl, struck it with the beater and made circular strokes around the rim.

The first chink heralded a cascade of droning notes. They filled the room, finding and forming warm structures in the black, musty air. The sound was intense, loud, smooth, invisible. I followed the beats as they rippled through each other. I concentrated on the gaps as they grew steadily smaller, until eventually they disappeared completely, and one note rang true in the dark. I succumbed once more, transported into a hypnotic sense of unity and perfection. I was content, held and drawn by this sound, this music that gained depth and degree with every eurhythmic turn of my arm. Its soft fingers reached into me. I was more alert this time. I was able to think and feel, to watch and hear more clearly. This one note was a template, a template for every conceivable sound that could ever be. It contained everything my ears could ever hear, arranged in a pattern of absolute harmony and concord. I was captivated, lost in time, frozen in a moment of eternal becoming. I stopped thinking.

My arm began to slow. The note dipped and dived in waves. My arm moved more and more slowly until it stopped. The bowl was on the floor; my hands hung at my sides. I imagined I was somewhere distant, watching myself from afar. Someone else was present, and the note was all around me in the blackness. Some words sprang to my mind:

It fetters the human body to the mind, gluing them together with the stuff of the soul, a continuous but unheard vibration.

My first impulse was to reach out and pick up the bowl, but I restrained myself. I dared not move in case the sound stopped. Time was an entity that flowed elsewhere and affected other things, tethering them to the artificial stepping-stones of moments. No friendly hand would come to reconnect me with its tides this time. On this occasion I was disturbed by something else altogether. It began with a vague sense of foreboding, an intimation of a threat that threaded the gaps back into the fabric of time. It worked against my will, invading the atmosphere I had created for myself in the heart of the mountain. And yet it came from within me, rising up from channels that I hadn't known existed. I could not identify it, but it was gaining strength.

I heard a different sound. It was my breath, rasping like sandpaper in my dry mouth. My muscles were contracting, twitching. I was panicking, and I couldn't move. I was still watching myself from somewhere in the blackness. And someone was watching me watching myself: I sensed a presence. I opened my eyes, and although I couldn't see anything, I was sure there was another man in the cave. I felt the brush of his beard against my cheek. He was standing over me, whispering into my ear. I tried not to listen, but I couldn't keep his words away much longer. I was paralysed by fear. A bead of sweat rolled from my forehead, gathered on my chin, hung there for an eternity then fell free. I saw it fall from across the room, slowly drifting to the ground, freezing an inch above the rock, pausing as if to ponder its fate before crashing with a tremendous peal of thunder on the cave floor. Then everything changed.

Fire! People screaming. Torches, houses set alight. Men, women and children trapped and terrified. I see their faces as the fire flickers closer, feel the heat as it scorches their skin. The air is thick with the stench of burning flesh and I am overwhelmed by pity and sorrow and guilt. Why guilt?

In the chaos, ceilings fall, floors turn to flame, walls crumble. People are screaming, trapped in the raging heat. Fire: the element of sudden change, sign of the dragon, bringer of death I race through the city with the mob. From house to house we run with fire in our hands, selecting targets and delivering them to hell. On victim-doors I see the mark: the accursed triangle of dots. I race on. The fire is everywhere. It surrounds me.

Through the smoke I see familiar faces, dying in the raging holocaust. Through the screams I hear a name. It is my name. They are calling me but I am helpless, trapped in crackling flame. I am ablaze. I am burning. I am dying. I roar a primeval death-yell into the air and collapse on the cold granite floor, shaking, shivering, sweating, weeping.

The vision abated: Cold air. Silence. Dark stillness.

I feel the heat. I see the faces. I see the mark: a triangle of dots. What does it mean? My ears are screaming. My leg is burning. My pocket is burning with real heat. I reel over onto my back and struggle to empty it, panicking, conscious only of the memory of fire and flame. An object falls, strikes the floor and rolls out of reach. I freeze. The burning sensation has gone. My fingertips hurt. All I hear is my breath, like the rasp of a reptile reverberating around the cave. In the terrifying blackness I scrabble to find the candle and matches.

The first match failed.

    The second match broke.

        The third match had already been used.

The fourth match roared into life. The gentle yellow light of the candle flooded the cave and I could see once more. The silk package that Ch'ien gave me was lying on the floor in the far corner. I stared for some time, cautious, afraid. Picking it up, I carefully removed the layers of silk. They were surprisingly cool. A pendant fell out, just like the one I'd had. I didn't need to roll it over to know what was etched onto the smooth ivory. I felt it like Braille beneath my fingers, a triangle of dots: one, two, three, then four.

I awoke outside the cave with no memory of how I'd got there, trembling with cold, wet with dew. My mind was addled. I didn't recognise my thoughts. I was hungry, thirsty, and my legs were cut and bruised from scrambling out of the cave. The fingertips of my left hand were blistered. I crawled to my bag, drank the flask of iced tea, ate two packets of rice then lay on the ground staring up at the empty sky. Dawn was breaking. The noises of the jungle: clicks and rustles; the hollow echo of water droplets from the cave, a flapping of wings, the gentle lapping of a distant river on wooden hulls, the rumble of a faraway ocean, the rumble of the earth. I lay there for hours without a single thought passing through my head, until eventually one rose up from the lower levels of my consciousness and presented itself: I'd put the prayer bowl on the floor of the cave – *I'd put the prayer bowl on the floor of the cave*. And yet the music had endured! How long could a note reverberate in such a tiny place before it faded and died, muffled by the immensity of the mountain? To what extent had my impression of time been distorted as I sat circling my arm around the rim, descending into ever-deepening levels of concentration?

'*Musica humana*', I had said to Ch'ien after my first experience of the cave. The words had rung true, but it was hardly an explanation. I sat up, crossed my legs, closed my eyes and listened closely to the pulse of the world. Amongst the chaotic warbling of nature's melodies, I tried to find the note from the cave. I caught glimpses, but I couldn't hold it. I was distracted by whispers in the back of my mind, whispers I didn't understand and a vivid feeling that I was being watched. I opened my eyes and scanned the edge of the clearing, but I didn't expect to find anything.

Eventually I rose from the floor and left the entrance of the cave. I avoided Ch'ien's village and the road and headed straight to Phongsali. From there I hitchhiked to Hat Xa and waited for the next boat heading south.

Nam Ou

The slowboat passed sedately through the gurgling waters of the winding *Nam Ou*. Huge trees reached out from the riverbank, the vivid green lustre of their leaves reflected perfectly in the gently moving water, so perfectly that the dividing line between the river and the land was barely visible. The sky poured a pale tropical blue between the branches. I was trailing one finger in the water, mesmerised by the shimmering reflections.

Our engine had failed several miles upriver and we were coasting downstream, gliding at the water's pace to the nearest sizeable village, silent, slow and calmly drifting. The pilot had assured us he would be able to arrange the necessary repairs and we'd be able to continue the journey later in the day. I didn't mind. I was in no hurry. Every so often we'd pass tiny villages, far too small to be of any assistance. Children worked with their parents in the shallows, washing hair and clothes, spearing unseen prey, casting nets or collecting freshwater shrimp from the riverbed. When our slowboat drifted into view, they'd all stop what they were doing and stare at our strange faces: one Japanese, two bearded Israeli, a red-headed American, two English and a blonde Norwegian. Some of them initially looked scared, some bold, others statuesque in their feigned indifference. When they turned to their parents and found reassurance in their relaxed smiles, the boys turned to greet our waving hands with unbridled enthusiasm, leaping around in the water, dancing and shouting, pulling faces and yelling at us with joy. They were probably showing off for the young girls who stood calmly watching us, smiling broadly and waving almost as an afterthought. Every time we passed one of these villages, we struggled out of our cramped positions to wave and smile at the children. The boat was always more animated and lively afterwards, but the heat of the sun and the soporific gurgling of the river inevitably sent our thoughts inward. We'd turn to contemplation, dangling our fingers in the water, watching reflections, snapping open sunflower seeds, listening to the sounds of the nearby jungle, reading books or just staring out at the world as time passed us slowly by.

In my hand I held the new pendant Ch'ien had given me. I often caught myself caressing the pattern of dots, seeking to understand them by the touch of my fingertips, hoping to sense an underlying meaning that my eyes failed to see. I found no other marks, no other inscription. I was tempted to smash it in the hope that another clue might reveal itself. I didn't.

Keep it with you always and you shall not want for friends.

The boat drifted with the current and my mind drifted too, gliding into empty spaces where it idled in the tropical heat.

It was nearly dark when we reached a village large enough to undertake repairs, and it was clear we would not be leaving until the next day. The pilot and his crew drank coffee with friends, sharing news and discussing the faulty engine. Food was being prepared but I wasn't hungry. I borrowed a lantern and wandered off.

Three months had passed since my stay in Ch'ien's bamboo grove. I'd spent all that time travelling in Laos, mostly on the rivers, on the move, never staying more than a couple of nights in one place. I'd travelled to the more remote parts of the country: to the north and east, often on my own or sometimes with locals who used the rivers to ply their wares and reach their fields. I enjoyed my inability to communicate, preferring the warm smiles and essential gestures to the endless small talk of western pleasure-seekers. I had to undertake the obligatory visa runs to the Thai border, and was on one now, riding the Nam Ou south towards the Mekong and Chiang Khong.

I'd ceased dreaming altogether, which surprised me. For three months my nights had been filled with tiny flashes of light in an otherwise featureless landscape of sleep. Sometimes I'd remember single colours, and the entry in my journal would read simply 'blue-green', 'just white', or 'silver-grey'. Most of the time there was nothing at all to record. During this period, every day at dusk and dawn I adopted the habit of wandering off on my own and spending at least an hour sitting quietly by the riverbank. I'd take my journal and leave it open on a blank page, then close my eyes and start listening: the sound water makes when it laps against the bank or slaps the underside of a canoe, the sloshing of eddies in the shallows, the burbling of rapids further upstream, the gulping noise of a rock moving. Rivers are great facilitators of deep concentration, even more so when they're accompanied by the percussive drone of the jungle cicadas. For the first few months I took the prayer bowl on these solitary walks. After an interval of ten to fifteen minutes, I'd lift the bowl, tap the rim and circle my arm. After a similar interval, the ambient sounds grew distant and I was able to hold my focus on the note that came from the bowl. I focussed inward, visualising the sound arising from the base of my spine, welling up through my body to my mind. I was searching out the subtle music of the cave. I wrote notes in the journal, but more often, the page remained blank.

It took a month of this routine to regain the slightest glimpse of what the sensation had been, but I recognised it immediately. I recognised the distracting whispers too. They arrived just before the music, a rustling of leaves that pulled my attention, holding me back. After the second month, I found I no longer needed the prayer bowl, as I knew where to go in my mind. But I could still only find echoes of earlier experiences, rather than anything real and present. I tried not to dwell on the fiery visions I had had on my second visit to the cave. They brought pain, the pain of others.

I walked along the Nam Ou until the noises from the village became inaudible and sat by a wide bend in the river. A gentle wind blew along the valley. The sky was clear and full of stars. As I began my meditations, a noise made me open my eyes. It sounded like a foot crunching loudly, on leaves. I had that feeling of paranoia you sometimes get when you wake up in the middle of the night having failed to draw breath, convinced that something sinister has broken into your dreams. I looked around, scanning the tree line, though I knew in my heart that I'd not see anything. It was the whispers, not the leaves. I focussed on the cicadas and relaxed. The water gurgled. A mosquito buzzed nearby. I closed my eyes and the whispers were there again. I held my focus. I waited for them to subside. I caught a glimpse of the music. It slipped away and the whispers grew louder. I silenced them – they would not come back – and the music welled up and washed over me. A rippling current ran up and down my spine, tingling the base of my skull. Tickling vibrations quivered my heart and lungs. I imagined it as how purring feels to a cat. My perception of time fell away and I felt warm and light. It was almost exactly like the initial experience of the cave, before the strange visions of fire and flame had ruined things, except I could now end it when I wished. I was detached, free to feel, probe, taste and savour.

I opened my eyes and consulted my watch. Three and a half hours had elapsed. I felt alert, refreshed. The contrast with the aftermath of both of my cave experiences couldn't have been more profound. I had not been overwhelmed or exhausted, and I had wilfully pulled away from the entrancing glow. Ch'ien had said he had no more to tell me, through unwillingness or a lack of knowledge, I wasn't sure which. I still had his letter to Thon in my bag. I was heading for Thailand and Chiang Khong, intending to come straight back to Laos with a new visa, but I changed my plans. I needed to find out what was happening, and Thon was the only person I could think of who might help. I needed to get back to Chiang Mai.

The next day I abandoned the unreliable slowboat and chartered a speedboat. There are many of these incongruous beasts hurtling up and down the Mekong: sleek, stylised dragracers that fly over the water at tremendous speeds, dodging rocks and shooting over the shallows – at full speed they almost lift off the water and fly. To my amazement, my luck failed with the engine again, and I found myself stranded in a village even smaller than the one where I had abandoned the slowboat. There were no roads and I was only half-way to the border at Chiang Khong. Despite my protests, the pilot was adamant we would not be leaving that day, so I sought lodgings. I found a bed in a small home-stay with two rooms, each with a window facing out across the Mekong. They were, in fact, one room, divided by a flimsy wicker wall. Someone was shuffling around on the other side, and I couldn't ignore the distraction. I tried to meditate but gave up and gazed out of the window, idly plucking my guitar. I hadn't played it much, but still carried it with me. As my fingers moved, my thoughts wandered to Chiang Mai and the friend I was eager to return to. A few moments passed before a light rapping on the door interrupted me. The shuffling had stopped in the other room. I went to the door.

Clever Glass Windows

'Hello.'

'Hello.'

'I'm Max.'

'Sebastian.'

His name didn't ring any bells, but I felt sure I'd seen him somewhere. We faced each other across the threshold of my room for a few seconds. I was waiting to hear what he wanted, but he said nothing, simply stared at me. I invited him in and he went to sit at the end of the bed. I returned to the stool by the window.

'I heard you playing the guitar.'

His hands were fidgeting and he didn't look at me directly.

'Do you play?'

'No, not really. I used to'

Silence again. We were punctuating it with awkward words and I felt it was my turn to speak.

I recalled the silhouette of a dreadlocked stranger I'd glimpsed once when approaching Thon's house in Chang Mai. I had seen him again in Laos, in the guesthouse before I took the boat up to Luang Nam Tha. He'd arrived there late at night, I was sure of it.

'I'm sure I recognise you. Have we met before?'

'Er, I don't think so. I...'

His voice tailed off. He was staring at my chest – at the pendant with the triangle of dots on that Ch'ien had given me.

'You recognise the pendant?' I asked.

'Yes.'

'Where from?'

He pulled a similar pendant from his tee-shirt. His manner seemed hesitant and uncertain. 'I've seen you around, but I hadn't noticed the pendant until you walked up from the river earlier. I didn't recognise you at first.'

Recognise me from where? He can't possibly have seen me clearly in Chiang Mai, and I could only have been a shadowy figure on the balcony in Chiang Khong, – not somebody to recognise.

'In this part of the world you keep meeting the same people.'

Was he following me or was I paranoid? I had spent a lot of time on my own, and I couldn't deny the peculiarity of the whispers in my head, but this little village on the Mekong was hardly on the beaten track. I wasn't sure which was worse: being followed or being paranoid.

'So why did you stop playing music?'

He seemed relieved by my choice of question. 'I studied it quite intensely and I suppose it lost some of its charm. Are you travelling back to Thailand tomorrow or heading further into Laos?'

'Thailand, if the engine is working.'

'I need to head back as well, my visa's run out. I got here overland though, if you can believe it.'

'I chartered a speedboat and I'm the only one in it. It should be fixed and ready to go by tomorrow morning, so there's room if you want...'

'What about cash? I can pay you when we get to Chiang Khong.'

'No need – I've paid already and I'll be going whether you come with me or not.'

I could hear the sound of the Mekong lapping in the wake of a stealthy canoe. Mosquitoes were buzzing. Darkness was falling, so I lit a couple of candles and an incense stick. Max waited for me to finish my housekeeping.

'Tell me why you gave up music, Max.'

He took a deep breath, looked me square in the eye for the first time, then spoke. He seemed nervous and I noticed he didn't answer the question I'd asked. 'I'm no good at stories, although I do talk well enough when I get going, so I'm told. Anyway, I don't really know who you are – but I'm friends with a guy in Chiang Mai who described you to me.'

'Thon?'

'Yes.'

'Do you know him well?'

'Not really, I suppose. I went to University with a friend of his in Canada.'

'Natalia?'

'Yes. You know her?'

'Only what Thon's told me.'

'I haven't seen her for a long time, but I see Thon every now and then. We talk sometimes. Well, I suppose I talk and he listens.'

'Go on.'

'Well, he didn't tell me much about you; just that you were a friend of his and that if we ever bumped into each other, we'd probably get along. I've got some ideas I'm playing around with – from my studies. I can't figure out what he thinks about them to be honest. He keeps his opinions to himself most of the time. At least he does with me.'

'I'm sure if Thon couldn't help, I certainly won't be able to,'

'He said I should talk to you if I got the chance… Do you fancy a beer? I've got a couple of bottles in my room. I'll get them.'

When he came back he was armed with a notepad and two bottles of Beer Lao.

'What do you know about the history of music? About its beginnings?' he asked. His voice had changed. It was more animated, more confident in tone, sharper in pitch.

'A little.'

'Every culture, no matter how isolated, uncivilised, weird or wonderful, uses music of some sort, so music must arise of its own accord, independent of circumstance or location. It pops up, like language, but how it arises is often quite different. Pick any culture you like and I'll give you an example.'

'Anywhere?'

'Anywhere.'

'Europe.'

'By which you mean Greece, my speciality?'

'Do I?'

'Yes. And we're talking numbers. Do you know the Pythagorean magic triangle – the three-four-five right-angled triangle?'

'I do.'

'The magic triangle was one of the foundations of mathematical science. When it was first conceived it carried a huge mythical and metaphysical significance. It was thought of literally as a *magical* triangle – one of several symbols for the fundamental forms of the natural world, a testament to man's ability to decode the order of the world and understand the patterns of creation.'

'So what's it got to do with music?'

Music of Maninjau – 127

'Music needs something to anchor itself to. Individual musicians usually use middle C. Orchestras usually use A. The choice seems quite arbitrary, so much so that for hundreds of years classical composers instructed their orchestras to tune to quite different frequencies, all of which were called A, but were probably closer to a B.'

'Why?'

'They used to raise the pitch to make their pieces sound brighter than everyone else's. Imagine it – composers everywhere nudging up the notes into higher and higher frequencies in a bid to out-do each other. If they hadn't put a stop to it, we'd be making music for cats and dogs by now!

'But let's consider C. Did you know that for a long time composing in the key of C was considered blasphemous? C was the perfect key – the key of God, no sharps or flats. Daft really. Tell me, what notes are in a C major chord?'

'C, E and G.'

'And the intervals describe the Magic Triangle. Here I'll draw it.'

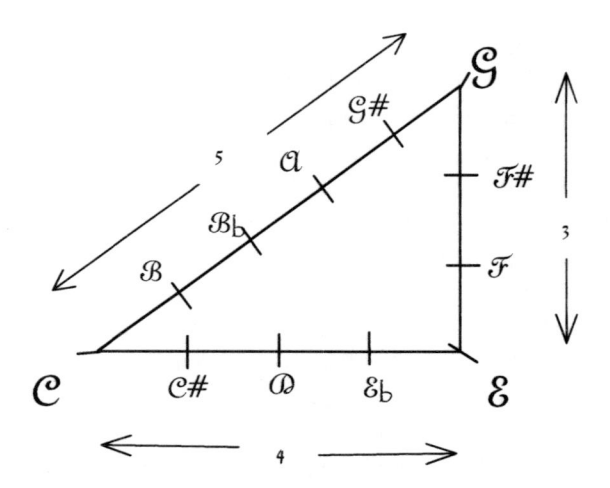

'If you look at the diagram, between the notes of C and E there are four semitones - and between the E and the G, three. Between the G and the next C – an octave higher than where we began – there are five semitones. Three, four, five: the intervals of the C major chord describe the magical triangle! Or does the magical triangle describe the C major chord?

'There are twelve notes in the chromatic scale, and twelve unit steps around the triangle. The triangle is an octave, and the corners define the notes of the major chord. Which inspired the other – music or mathematics? Does one merely *describe* the other? If so, which one? Do they arise independently and are just coincidentally synchronous? Perhaps they both describe something bigger and more complex, something they can only partially render separately. Maybe they are like languages that happen to overlap, languages created to communicate ideas beyond sound and number?' He leaned back on his chair, looking pleased with himself. I was slightly bewildered by the barrage of unanswered questions.

'Like what?'

'That's the tricky bit, but I have a neat way of describing it. Imagine this: imagine a room contained within a room. The inner room is spherical and has many small windows. On the outside of this room – in the outer room – chairs face the windows, one chair per window. There is a person on every chair and each can only see through their own window. In the centre of the inner room there is a single object. Can you see the arrangement?'

'I think so. What's the object?'

'I'm coming to that. Each window is made from a different material. All of them distort the view. No two windows distort the same way. Not only do shapes change, but colour, sheen, texture... The windows even transmit and distort sound and smell as well. Only one characteristic escapes change: the object is inherently beautiful. This is the only characteristic common to all who view it. Are you with me?'

'I thought beauty was supposed to be in the eye of the beholder?'

'What difference does it make? If you'd prefer, we could just say that all the people *behold* an object of beauty when they look through their window. The glass exaggerates whatever it is that the viewer beholds as beautiful. They're *clever glass windows*, okay? They know who's looking through them, and they change their properties accordingly.'

'Millions of humans at millions of windows, no windows are the same, no view is the same, but the object – whatever it may be- is inherently and *objectively* beautiful! Or is *perceived as beautiful* by every one of them. I'm with you Max, I think.'

'It's more beautiful than anything they have ever seen or could ever conceive of.'

'Okay.'

'So, the people are left to watch the object for a while and then they are all dumped into a third room where they discuss the nature of what they have just seen through their own personal window. Discuss? – I mean argue. They speak passionately about the object because they were all so moved by its beauty. Some people refuse to accept that their description is not the correct one. They shout louder to impose their will. Others form groups who reach a kind of consensus because their ideas overlap enough to force a compromise. This doesn't resolve the problem though – it just creates factions. Fights break out. People rant about the vanity of ideas, but stubbornly refuse to question their own – it's chaos.

'Occasionally, a solitary figure might pass unnoticed through the mayhem and quietly listen to what everybody else is saying. He just listens and learns. He sees the fragments. He perceives the trick. He understands the relativity. Who is he? He's a true philosopher, but that isn't the important thing for us.

'Sitting somewhere in amongst the jostling crowd, are musicians and mathematicians. Both can use their ideas – their *language* – to render something fundamental and universal about the beautiful object. They find an audience easily because their descriptions are intelligent, accessible and well articulated. The ideas overlap with each other, so they can combine to develop an even more vivid metaphor. Am I making sense?'

I had just lifted the bottle of Beer Lao to my lips as he asked the question. By the time I'd taken it away again, he'd already moved on.

'You know, Liebnitz said music is *mathematics for souls who don't know they are calculating*. It's a clever definition. Do you know what Einstein had to say about the matter?'

'No.'

'*If I were not a physicist, I would probably be a musician. I often think in music. I live my daydreams in music. I see my life in terms of music.* And he was a mathematical genius. Nowadays you wouldn't get away with it so easily – putting music anywhere near mathematics in a sentence, I mean. You'd get called a philistine or people would just look at you as if you were mad or just lacking in soul. It wasn't always like that though. When the idea of the geometric triangle was first proposed, and the major chord understood not long after, it must have been mind-blowing. Imagine the excitement of relating the two together like they did. But it was kept secret for a long time.'

He took a much-deserved swig of his beer, his eyes burning with an intensity that forbade interruption. He drank quickly, then hammered the bottle down on the table, causing a crown of bubbles to pour out of the top.

I was enjoying myself.

'The popular myth of where our laws of harmony come from is the anecdote about Pythagoras overhearing a blacksmith striking metal. Supposedly, he heard different notes as the hammer struck, recognised the intervals and figured it all out properly when he got home, using pieces of string and some bricks. Bunkum…'

'Bunkum?'

'Exactly. I think it was all far more deliberate and far more profound than the anecdote would have us believe. I think Pythagoras' leap of genius lay in discovering the concept of *harmony*, the idea that things can come together in harmonious or dissonant ways; that things work better if they have harmony woven into the fabric of their being. It applies to music in an obvious and straightforward way, but it also applies to everything that happens in the natural world: to the way crystals form, to the way water flows down a plughole, to the way atoms fuse or clouds release their rain. It applies to the way stars and solar systems grow. Why do galaxies take their shape? Because it's the only form that offers stability, harmony. This quality is in fact the process by which the mundane grit of the universe joins itself together to make patterns of ever-increasing complexity. Life is high harmony. The heavens, whatever they might be, have even higher harmony. There's more to this than just anvils and hammers.

'*Music is a revelation; a revelation loftier than all wisdom and philosophy,*' he quoted.

'But perhaps no greater than mathematics. Where's that from?'

'Beethoven, I think.'

'Clever man.'

I knew it was Beethoven, but not for the first time in recent months, I was surprised I knew. Had I read about him and subsequently forgotten all but a few snippets?

Max continued, 'Mathematics and the theory of music were the two ways Pythagoras chose to explain this. Out of one window came sound, and out of another came numbers. He was a true philosopher.'

'So you're saying the object in the room is harmony? Where did beauty go?' I was puzzled.

'*I* can't say what is in the room, because I can't look through all the windows. Like everyone else, I've only got one window. Harmony is closely tied to beauty. As you said before, it's in the eye of the beholder.'

'I suppose it is.'

'And mathematics and music were ways to describe what he saw and understood. Study the two and you study the object as well as you can.'

'It sounds like something else to me,' I said, playing the devil's advocate.

'What? God? I don't like the word.'

I could tell by his tone he was sincere.

'Why not?'

'Look, harmony is another way of saying things exist *just so*. The petals of a flower only exist as they do because all the component parts – chemical, physical, electrical and nuclear – work together in a harmonious way. Human beings are harmonic. The universe is staggeringly harmonic. If God exists, He must surely be *perfectly* harmonic, neatly implying that He creates, is composed of, and encompasses, all things.'

'Didn't the Greeks have a bickering pantheon of gods?'

'They were studying metaphysics. Deep down they must have known it was bunkum.'

I finished my Beer Lao. Max blew the foam off the top of his bottle and drank some more. He was barely halfway through and what was left was probably warm. Veins stood out on either side of his forehead and he was out of breath from talking. I offered to go and get more beer.

The owners of the home-stay were sitting in front of the television watching a game show. I recognised the format from English television. They were utterly absorbed. I had difficulty getting their attention, but eventually they sold me a few more Beer Laos. When I returned, Max had finished his beer and was standing by the window. He went back to the bed and proffered his key-ring bottle opener.

'So you said all this to Thon?' I asked.

'Yes, and a lot more besides. I've only dug you half a warren so far.'

'And?'

'I couldn't figure out if he just didn't get it and stayed quiet, or if he was being deliberately silent for some other reason. Sometimes he just doesn't say anything, regardless of what you say to him. Depends on his mood, I reckon. It's refreshing to find somebody who wants to listen. As I've already said, if you mention music and mathematics in the same sentence, musicians will treat you like a leper, while mathematicians just appear slightly amused.'

'Can I ask you another question, Max?'

'Sure.'

'Where did you get your pendant?'

'Huh?'

'The pendant with the dots.'

'I'm not sure. Cambodia, I think.'

'Not Malaysia?'

'I haven't been there. Why?'

'You've never been to George Town?'

'I've never been to Malaysia. I presume George Town is in Malaysia. Is that where you got yours?'

'Yeah.' It wasn't strictly true: Ch'ien had given it to me, but it was identical to the one I'd bought in George Town.

'I definitely got mine in Cambodia. I was surprised to see another one to be honest, that's why I was looking at yours. Thon's got one too.'

'I haven't seen it.'

'He's got one. I've seen the same pattern on his door as well. To be honest, I only bought it for the inscription. I didn't want the dots. I'd certainly never decorate my door with them.'

'Do you know what they represent?'

'No, you?'

'No.' He opened his beer. The lid rattled across the table and stopped. Our eyes followed it.

'So, how much of the warren is there left to dig?' I asked.

'You want to hear more?'

'Sure, why not?'

'You're a good audience, probably the best I've had. Except for Thon obviously, but it's nice to have a bit of input as well as a good pair of ears every now and then. If you get tired, just say the word.'

'I'm fine.'

'Okay, back to the numbers. In the C Major chord, C to E is an interval of four semitones, C to G is seven and C to the octave is twelve. That's four, seven and twelve. In another process, completely separate from the development of musical theory, humankind sat down one day and imposed a discrete structure on time. What did we get? Twelve hours in a day, twelve in a night, seven days a week, four weeks in a lunar month, twelve calendar months in a year, four seasons...'

'But they don't add up! What about leap years?'

'Leap years occur every *four* years, near as dammit. And

besides, the musical scales don't fit together perfectly either. Who knows, maybe the errors in the numbers of music match up with the errors in all of our observations of natural harmony. I don't know. Regardless of which came first though, the same patterns are there. Spiritual and religious numerology is riddled with it: seven archangels, twelve apostles, the twelve pipes of *lus*, seven…'

'The twelve pipes of *lus*!'

'Chinese. Talking about religion though, the interval of six …'

'Wait, you said the twelve pipes of *lus*. What do you know about them?' If he knew about the *lus* pipes, it was possible that he knew of them through the same channel as I did: Ch'ien. He already knew Thon, and he had one of the mysterious pendants around his neck. Perhaps he had been in the cave.

'I think the holy men used them. They were sacred in old China. The interval of six, though – you get it by cutting the octave in half. It's the most dissonant interval in the chromatic scale, it stinks. Jazz musicians use it all the time, but for a long time it was despised.'

'*Musica in diabolus.*'

'Exactly. And six just happens to be the numeral most associated with evil, and the Devil. Nobody sat down and put all of this together. There wasn't a plan; it just happened. It's inside us, waiting to get out, but only because it's everywhere, always.'

'What about the pipes – the *lus* pipes?'

'What? The *lus* pipes? I don't know. Instruments are just instruments, and even sacred pipes are just pipes. What's important is that the Chinese thought they were special, whether they were or not, and, hey presto, they made twelve of them instead of eleven or thirteen, or six or two.'

I took from this that he had not met Ch'ien, which made me feel both relieved and disappointed. I desperately wanted to talk to somebody about what I was feeling, what I had experienced in the cave and what I was now able to summon in just ten to fifteen minutes of quiet reflection. Since leaving the cave, the time and effort needed to relive the experience had gradually diminished. I presumed that there might come a time when I would not have to commit any effort at all. Would I live with it always? Would I grow used to it and no longer notice it? Or would it enrich me with the same intensity? If it did, would I be able to cope with my life, feeding and clothing myself? I was distant from such demands when the soft shawl of the mysterious *musica humana* wrapped around me. The first time I had experienced it, three days had passed without the slightest awareness of hunger or fatigue. I needed to get back to Thon.

'Sebastian?'

I'd drifted away.

'Yes, Max. Sorry, I am listening.'

'I thought I'd lost you.'

'No, I'm following you. You were talking about numerology. But surely that's all it is? It's not even mathematics, never mind music.'

'They're clues. I could give you more sophisticated mathematical examples: the Fibonacci series or applied fractal theories. Or scientific ones: we are told now that everything is made up of the same tiny strands of energy, or matter, or whatever you want to call it. They obey the same rules for joining together. Understand these rules, and you understand everything that proceeds from them. It's the Holy Grail of theoretical scientists: the grand unified theory, a theory of all the forces that hold sway in the universe. Regardless of how or why it happens, it is inevitable that these tiniest strands of existence will come together as they do and form, amongst other things, this galaxy, this planet, this continent, this room, the beer in my hand – and me. Understand harmony in its fullest sense and all of the clever glass windows will be smashed, no matter how complex and weighty they may have become.'

'And what do scientists make of this theory?'

'Huh?'

'Scientists. How would a particle physicist respond to this?'

'I don't really care. They're too busy metaphorically shooting themselves in their metaphysical feet.'

'What?'

'An example: no experiment can ever be carried out in true isolation. They call that *nonlocality*. What they mean is that every single speck of dust in the universe is connected to every other. An electron in the sun could theoretically nudge my Bunsen burner when I'm minding my own business trying to figure out what the hell an electron is. And the electron! – we can never know where one is and at the same time know where it's going – they call that *Heisenberg's uncertainty principle*. Surely that makes things a little messy? No? How about the idea that even if you simply look at an electron, you change the way it behaves? You can't look without touching. As soon as you put it under the microscope, it runs away. Same principle. Uncertainty? Nobody's ever even seen an electron, all we see are the puffs of cloud they leave behind. Everything is inference and abstraction. This isn't description, it's an accumulation of grease and oil on the clever glass windows. To make matters worse, the grease guns are in the hands of bankers and corporations who couldn't care less about what's behind the windows. They just want more efficient batteries and cheaper lasers for their compact discs.

Science has cut its own arms off. It's just a lumbering pit pony, shifting coal for its corpulent masters and going blind in the process. It's forgotten where it came from and what it's for.'

'What's this got to do with music, Max?'

'Huh?'

'Music, Max. Harmony and Beauty?'

I was losing the thread, trying to follow his arguments whilst part of my mind was trying to tie in my recent experiences since the cave with all he had told me about Pythagoras and his theories of harmony.

'Mathematicians and musicians used to be friends. Then they drifted part. They spent some time standing at opposite ends of the room shouting at each other. Nowadays they don't even bother. They're both shackled. Most music is more like the bread you get in a supermarket than the symbolic bread you find in a church. It's everywhere, but everywhere you look it's losing track of its purpose.'

'Have you read Lu Bu We, Max?'

'Lu Bu who?'

'We, Lu Bu We.'

'Never heard of him.'

I rooted through my bag and found the book I'd bought in Bangkok. It was frayed at the edges by now and some of the pages were loose, but I still carried it. I flicked to the back and found Lu Bu We. I passed it to Max and told him to read two highlighted passages:

> *The cause of the degeneration of the Chu State was its invention of 'magic music'. Because it departed from the essence of real music, the music was not serene. All of this arises from mistaking the nature of music and seeking only tempestuous tonal effects.*

When the world is at peace, when all things are tranquil, then music can be perfected. When desires and passions do not turn into wrongful paths, music can be perfected. Perfect music has its cause. It arises from equilibrium. Equilibrium arises from righteousness, and righteousness arises from the meaning of the cosmos. Therefore, one can speak about music only with a man who has perceived the meaning of the cosmos.

'Can I borrow this?'

'Of course. I'd say you've found a friend.'

'Uncanny. When was it written?'

'I've no idea. It doesn't say and I haven't tried to find out. I think some of the pages might have fallen out.'

'I'll find out on the Internet.'

'You shouldn't cut yourself up so much about this stuff Max.'

'What do you mean?'

'I mean you should play music to learn about harmony, no matter how far-reaching your ideas of it are.'

'You think it's bunkum.'

'No, I'm just saying be careful. If it's not looking after you, then it isn't music. Science might well be in the grip of the bankers, but a particle accelerator costs a fortune, so it's hard to get to the cutting edge without their help. To make music, all you need is your body and your mind.'

'You might be right.'

'I need to sleep Max. Can we carry this on tomorrow?'

'Sure. Where are you headed after Chiang Khong? Are you going to Chiang Mai?'

'No. Isarn, then to the tea plantations. I'm helping out with the harvest.'

'Really?'

'Yeah, I get a good supply of cheap Oolong. Picking tea is good for thinking too.'

'Well I'll see you tomorrow anyway.'

'What time?'

'About eight.'

'I'll see you then.'

'Goodnight Max.'

'Goodnight Sebastian.'

He picked up the tattered book and left.

Sound and Light

I'm in a hall. Thousands upon thousands of people are jostling around me in a melee of motion. They're all chattering away like birds, passing indecipherable clicks and whistles back and forth. I can't understand anything. I can't even see where the walls of the hall are. The ceiling is thousands of miles up and endlessly wide. I'm helpless, like a winged bug trapped on the surface of a flowing river.

How much time has passed? Some of the people have stopped chattering. They're looking up. The sheer scale of what's there makes me nauseous. A stupendously big clock face is chiselled into the ceiling. Its arms are many hundreds of miles wide. With every movement of time, the rock is riven and reformed, issuing terrific peals of thunder. There are hundreds of them, counting out the years, the days, the hours, the minutes, the seconds, milliseconds, microseconds, nanoseconds, all the way down to the tiniest of all moments, which can't be seen or experienced. The second hand is swinging at a reassuring pace and I try to focus on it, but everything is speeding up. I switch my attention to the passing of years, watching them fade away with every gut-wrenching roar of rock – fashions, fads and fancies of bygone eras fall from the ripping scars in a rain of broken images. Though I recognise much of what I see in the confetti of years, it all mingles with words that I cannot understand. When I lose sight of them, I forget them.

In the west there is light, in the east a dark shadow. I am drawn to the shadow, in which I can discern the coming and going of ill-defined shapes and forms, like faces.

How much time has passed? The chattering is manic, hysterical. People are looking downwards. The movement is furious but fading, and gradually thins out. I have more space now. The noises fade too. Figures file away into a distant silence and I find myself alone beneath the skyscape of passing time. Stillness is a whistling wind.

On the eastern horizon the figure of an old man appears, approaching me. It takes hundreds of years, but in this strange land he arrives almost immediately. I know the contours of his face as if they are my own. His eyes are older than the world. His skin is translucent, his hair silver. The gown he wears seems to reach beneath the floor, wafting behind and below him. He stands next to me and stares back to the darkness from whence he came. I stare with him, but there's nothing to see. I feel calmer and safer in the silence. How long do we stare like this? He turns and looks at me. He's holding something. It glows in his hand. I step forward. He opens his hands. It looks like a golden jellyfish, gently pulsating. It is circular, but inside it there are different shapes, like triangles with soft edges. The old man is smiling like a child, his eyes suddenly transformed from ancient to nascent in a single blink. I am filled with love. I try to embrace him, but I can't quite reach. I take a step forward but I still can't reach. I stretch out my arms, straining my shoulders and my neck, but I still can't reach him. Every time I step towards him, the space between us increases. I am running to touch him. He doesn't move, but the space between us is growing faster than I can cover it. The stillness is growing, and it separates us by ever-increasing distances. His eyes glow brighter as he drifts further away. I'm sprinting, leaping, screaming, straining to reach him.

The rock of time ruptures, the ceiling falls, the earth rises, the vision fades.

I woke to a knock at the door. The pilot of the speedboat had come to tell me the repairs were done and we were ready to go. He was in a hurry; it was still only seven o'clock. I woke Max, got dressed and packed my things.

The owners of the home-stay had prepared breakfast. We ate in silence, still half-asleep, then trudged down to the riverbank and boarded the speedboat. The pilot had obviously taken the opportunity to give it a thorough service, as it flew much faster than before. The combination of the engine's roar and the exhilarating speed made any kind of conversation impossible, so we retired into our thoughts as we cut in and out of rocky islands and screamed past the slowboats.

We arrived at the border shortly after noon and crossed straight into Thailand. At the terminal we booked tickets on the next available buses. I had to settle for a delivery truck, as the bus to Chiang Rai had fallen apart on the way up and there wasn't another for several hours. Max booked a ticket to Thoeng on a fully-functional bus. When we both had our tickets in our hands, we sat on the kerb and watched the world go by. A toothless old man glided by on a worn-out bicycle, smiling at us. Tuk-tuks gathered like flies, their drivers imploring us to let them take us somewhere. They kept asking, despite our repeated insistence that we were leaving the city. Occasionally a truck roared past and sent swirls of dust into the air, engulfing us in blinding pink clouds.

'When are you off?'
'Half an hour.'
'Fifteen minutes.'
'I'd better give you your book back.'

'Did you read much of it?'

'I was too tired.'

'Keep hold of it.'

'Are you sure?'

'Yeah. I'm sure. Who knows, we might meet again.'

He lit a cigarette. It was one of those travelling cigarettes you light when you're waiting for transport, have no desire to smoke, and very rarely enjoy.

'We've got quarter of an hour to kill. How much of the warren is there left to dig?'

'Are you serious?'

'Why not, we've got about…

I checked my watch.

'…twelve minutes.'

'It goes on forever; that's the problem with rabbit holes. There's one bit that ties in with what we spoke about last night though. I meant to mention it. It's about light.'

'Light?'

'Yeah.'

'Go on then – I'll be amazed if the transport arrives on time anyway.'

As I spoke those words, a truck flew past us, showering us in a storm of dust.

'Inside?' Max asked.

'I'll get the coffee; you get a table.'

Max had his notepad out again and was scribbling. He closed it when I sat down with the coffees.

'You'd better talk quickly, Max,' I told him as we stirred the white condensed milk into the thick black coffee.

'Okay. Sound and light both exist as narrow bands in an infinitely wide spectrum of energy: there's plenty we cannot hear or see, such as infrared light or ultrasonic sound. But even in the perceivable bands, there are an infinite number of colours and sounds, because the spectra have infinite depth as well as breadth.'

'Meaning?'

'How many times can you cut a piece of string in half?'

'Depends how small your knife is.'

'It's infinitely small. I think you're playing with me, which is daft because we've only got...'

'Nine minutes.'

'Then I'll presume you know. It's Zeno's paradox. Anyway...'

'But light is quantised – it comes in discrete little lumps with different energies.'

'Yes. But to all intents and purposes, no.'

'Why?'

'Because our eyes just aren't that good. The same could apply to noise. Noise is vibration and molecules only vibrate at discrete energies, but you'd never figure that out with just your ears. If you believe in string theory, then the smallest unit of vibration is inconceivably tiny. As far as we're concerned, and as far as our eyes and ears are concerned, the worlds of light and sound are continuous.'

'Okay.'

'From the audible continuum, we pulled out twelve sounds and called them the chromatic scale, but, finding that the intervals aren't always pleasing to the ear, we removed five. We then had seven: the diatonic scale – seven notes placed arbitrarily on the entire spectrum of sound and called the alphabet of European music. As you know, the major and the minor scales are both examples of diatonic scales. This is the legacy of the Greeks, and it is the historical basis of our music.'

'What about other cultures?'

'They've all found some of these notes, except Indonesian Gamelan, I think, but I don't know enough about that. It doesn't matter though – we'll stay with Europeans for the sake of getting through this before the truck comes in…'

'About eight minutes. You're talking quickly.'

'So, that's sound. What about light? Well, traditionally we've got seven colours in the visible rainbow, with an infinite array of shades and textures in between. Look at this.'

He flicked opened the notepad and turned to a page with a circle drawn on it. The twelve notes of the chromatic scale were written in the hour positions of a clock face, with the seven notes of the C-major scale written in bigger letters. On the inside of the clock, the seven colours of the rainbow correlated with the seven notes, with C represented by red, D with orange, and so on:

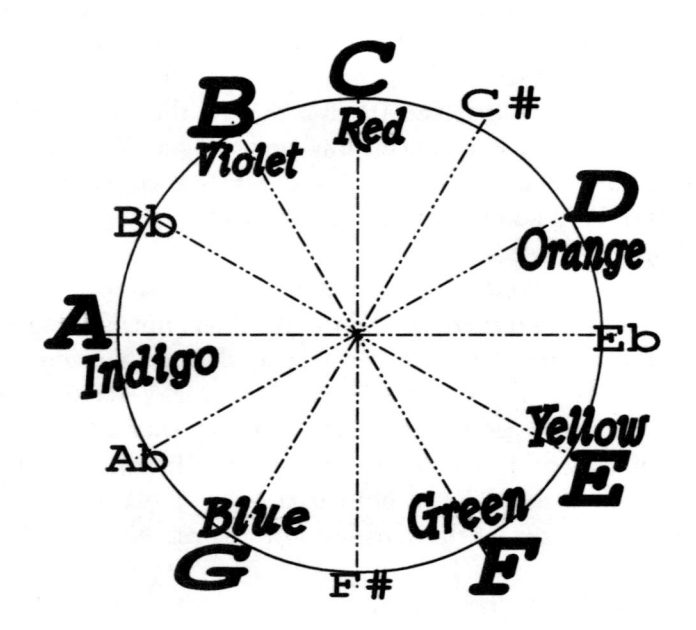

'I've chosen C arbitrarily, and assigned it the colour red because it has the lowest frequency of all the colours, so the frequencies of both the sound and light increase in a clockwise direction. Now, let's bring back the numbers quickly, but first: which note gets on best with the C?'

'The octave – a higher C.'

'Obviously. And then?'

'The fifth – G.'

'And then?'

'The fourth – F.'

'And then?'

'The third, E, I suppose.'

'And the mathematical ratios of these notes to the C are as follows.' He hastily scribbled a table onto the page, underneath the circle of notes and colours:

Note	C	G	F	E
Ratio	1:1	1:2	2:3	3:4

'We've been here before, linking the fundamentals of mathematics to the fundamental harmonies of music. Look at the numbers; 1:1; 1:2; 2:3; 3:4. That confirms what we already know. But look at the clock face of colour again. The first three notes of the table are represented by red, blue and green, the primary colours of light.'

'I thought the primary colours were red, blue and yellow.'

'In pigment they are, but not for light. Paints effectively remove colours from the spectrum of white light – red paint is red by virtue of being neither blue nor yellow nor green. It's red because when light hits the surface the only colour that isn't absorbed is red, so it bounces off and we see it. Think about it: if you keep on mixing paint, you always end up with black. If you keep on mixing light though, you'd get white. It's good that you mentioned it though: look what happens when you add the colours to the table:

Note	C	G	F	E
Ratio	1:1	1:2	2:3	3:4
Colour	Red	Blue	Green	Yellow

'The primary colours of light – red, blue and green – make up the major chord: C, G, F. The primary colours of pigment – red, blue and yellow – make up the minor chord: C, G, E. The building blocks of music, light and mathematics all working together. How long have we got?'

'Four minutes, just over. So what does it mean?'

'I don't know, but I like it. I like the fact that the world exists in this way. Maybe this means we've got three clever windows at our disposal? Maybe it brings the object a little closer?'

'What about octaves?'

'What do you mean?'

'When you go all the way around the clock, you get higher notes but they're still audible. What about the light?'

'You get ultraviolet. There might be distinct colours in the ultraviolet spectrum too. Why shouldn't there be? Light could have the equivalent of octaves.'

'Why should it?'

'Why couldn't it?'

We both finished our coffees.

'Have you heard of synaesthesia?' he asked, but gave me no time to answer as he continued, 'Some people see colours when they hear music. It's a blurring of the senses. An American guy wrote an orchestral piece called Bright Blue Music. The whole thing was in D major. People asked him why he didn't change key. He told them, 'I see blue when I listen to D major.'

'But according to your theory, D is orange. Are you saying he was colour blind?'

'Rimsky-Korsakov thought F-flat major was the blue key, whereas Skryabin swore it was a reddish purple. They had heated arguments about it, but they agreed with the theory, with the principle. It seems quite subjective, but I'm...'

A truck screeched to a halt outside, throwing massive clouds of D-major dust into the air, accompanied by the squeal and stink of pigs. The dust streamed through the window and engulfed the table. Impatient yells rang out amidst a sudden furore of activity. I saw my bag hurled into the back of the truck like a sack of garbage by the driver's mate. The old lady behind the counter pointed at me and I was surrounded by the chattering voices. Everything was chaotic and frenetic. A man had his hand on my arm, ushering me to my feet. I shook hands with Max and said a hasty 'goodbye and good luck', leapt into the rusty contraption and off we went. The floor was squirming with sacks of baby pigs and chickens with their legs tied together. I checked my watch: still two minutes to go.

I'm rushing through the memories of the world, finding fragments and holding them before they disintegrate into powder on the breeze of history. Sir Isaac Newton sits at his desk transcribing a circle into his notebook. The air around him is crackling with the laughter and ridicule of a host of ghostly bullies. He can't hear them. Time passes. The fragment fades.

Now I see Helmholtz. He casts his notebook into the fire with curses, storming back and forth with his hand on his chin, grimacing. I feel his frustration. The fragment fades.

Time passes, and hundreds of faces coalesce into the visage of Max. His brow is furrowed. He's standing in front of a canvas, trying to draw a million perfect circles. He can't finish any of them because the point at which he begins is constantly moving away from him. He can't join the lines up, so all he can draw is spirals. Infinite spirals that are indescribably massive and unbelievably small. He's sweating with the effort. His skin is aging. His hands shake and his shoulders hang. His hair grows fast and brittle and the nails on his fingers and toes curl up. When the fragment finally fades, he is unrecognisable.

Time passes. I see a round face staring at me. It's shouting something, but I can't make out what. All movement decays into static. The face is a mere silhouette in a blanket of stars. 'Chiang Rai!' *In the distance:* 'Chiang Rai!'

Thon

'Aie, farang!' The driver was shouting at me. 'Chiang Rai!'

He had reached into the back of the truck and was shaking me by the shoulder, trying to wake me up. But I wasn't asleep. His face was hidden in shadows, surrounded by stars. The sacks of whining piglets and the tethered chickens had gone and I was the only passenger left. I grabbed my pack and jumped out on uncertain legs. The driver went back to the cab, spat out of the open window, and drove off. The truck weaved up the road. I watched it turn a corner and disappear. My mind was filled with circles. The bus station was deserted except for a few rickshaw drivers who were leaning over their handlebars and talking in soft voices beside a crumbling wall. I called out to them, but they didn't respond. Where were the tuk-tuks? There were puddles everywhere, shining with oil and grease, reflecting the silver smile of the sideways moon. I climbed into the leather seat of the nearest rickshaw and spoke the name of the mechanic's workshop where I had left my bike several months earlier. The driver threw a half-hearted wave over his shoulder and took his time finishing his cigarette, listening to the quite whispers of his colleagues but not speaking himself. I listened too, but understood nothing. When the cigarette was done, he tossed the butt aside, turned the handlebars and silently pulled away from the throng. The soft voices disappeared, and all I could hear for a while was the crunch of the gravel beneath the slowly turning wheels. I curled up in my seat and watched the world slide by while the driver pedalled.

When I reached the workshop the mechanic offered me a room, making it clear that he expected no money in return. I thanked him, but refused, insisting that I had to travel that night. I paid him what I owed and said goodbye. He told me I was *not pineapple*, a colloquialism for being crazy. I kicked the starter and the machine erupted into life, the vibrations working their way through my flesh and into my weary bones. They shook me from my tiredness and gave me the strength to ride.

Chiang Mai was on fire when I arrived, filled to capacity with drunken tourists, glowing purple and red with the obscene neon buzz of the busy nightclubs. Honda Dreams and tuk-tuks swarmed on the roads and the smell of frying rice and noodles saturated the warm air. People were screaming at each other, waving bottles of Beer Chang and dancing through the streets. Young working women reached out from the bars with enticing hands, reeling in the foreigners to empty their wallets. It was late at night, or early the next morning. The debauched end of the tourist spectrum was in ascendance, and I had to pass right through the heart of it.

When I eventually pulled to a stop outside Thon's home, I felt a wave of relief. My bones were still vibrating with the rhythm of the motorbike and my hands had the warm numbness I always experienced on long rides. Thon's door was closed, but I heard his music. Advancing up the steps, I was raising my arm to knock when I noticed the symbol in the centre of the door: a tiny carving of the triangle of dots. I reached for my pendant and rubbed it between thumb and finger. A host of faces flew through my mind, some of which

I recognised, many of which I did not: the engraver, Ch'ien, Kur, Max, Nam, the lady of Lampun, Nathalia (though I'd never seen her face), a young girl that I barely recognised, a tall man in the robe of a monk, old men that seemed like brothers, faces that I thought were mine but on closer inspection were not, and Thon. The triangle of dots was clearly marked on the door. How had I failed to notice it? I let go of my pendant and knocked, but no answer came. The music played on uninterrupted, seeping through the cracks in the door and mingling with the bass thrum of the city. I pushed gently and the door swung open. Thon was sitting at the far end of the room, guitar nestled in his arms, fingers dancing lightly across the fretboard, eyes half-closed and eyelids flickering. His legs were crossed and the curve of his back swayed imperceptibly. I took a place opposite. Tired beyond reason, I lay down and slept.

Tiger balm: I felt its gentle sting on my forehead, temples and neck. I was lying on my back and my body was incredibly heavy. Thon was brewing tea. I heard the bubbling water and the whistle of the gas flame. I lifted my head, propping myself on one elbow, turning to face Thon. He was rolling his head to exercise his neck when he caught my movement out of the corner of his eye.

'Good morning Thon.'

'Good *afternoon* Sebastian. You slept well?' He poured tea into porcelain cups.

'I think so.'

'You were exhausted when you arrived last night, shaking and bleary-eyed.'

'I feel much better.'

'And you have much to tell me. How is old Ch'ien. Did you meet him? Is he well?'

I rubbed the remaining sleep out of my eyes, picked up a

wrap of coconut rice and told Thon everything that had happened. I told him about the *huang chung* and the prayer bowl and my first experience of the cave. He listened intently. I took the prayer bowl out of my bag and explained that I now needed neither the cave nor the bowl to recreate the experiences I had described. Recalling the surreal experience of the truck ride from Chiang Khong to Chiang Rai, I suspected that even meditation was unnecessary, but I said nothing of this to Thon. I told him about Max and his far-flung theories. I showed him the pendant and asked why the same symbol was etched on his door. I told him I had seen the same symbol in my dreams, and on the engraver's door.

'What *is* it, Thon?' I asked.

I sensed a hesitation. 'The symbol is called the Tetractys.'

'The what?'

'The Tetractys. The mark of an order. Used as a way of recognising friends.'

'What order?'

'A very old one, Sebastian. I am a member. Ch'ien is a member. The engraver you met in George Town must have been a member, though I do not know him. Max is also a member, though he may not yet realise the fact. You are a member.'

'What do you mean? '

'You have always been a member. You are born to it. Choice is irrelevant.' While I was taking in the implications of what he had said, he spoke again, 'Wait here a moment.'

'What for?'

'I have something for you. I'll only be a few seconds.'

He stood up, went into the back room, and returned with a small, battered, red book, which he placed in my hands. There was no title. I opened it, and on the first page, saw the triangle of dots. I was not surprised.

'Most of your questions should be answered by this book. You'll know some of it already, and what you don't know may sound familiar. Read it. Ask questions later.'

'What is it?'

'A collection of manuscripts. Some ancient, others less so. Some are only fragments. The sources are reliable. As with anything else, you must judge the value of the facts for yourself, but you can trust them.'

'Trust them?'

'History is not always reliable. It changes through the years. For us, the history books are wrong – all of them. This book will bring you closer to the truth.'

'What truth?'

'Trust me. I have business to attend to, so I will leave you with it. Please, read it. We can discuss it later. Don't be impatient, Sebastian. The book will explain itself. That is why we use it.'

He left. I sat alone in his room, staring at the uneaten wrap of coconut rice on the floor, flicking the brittle pages through my hands, dumbstruck and confused.

Part 3 – Musica Mundana

Music is in all growing things;
And underneath the silky wings
Of smallest insects there is stirred
A pulse of air that must be heard;
Earth's silence lives, and throbs, and sings.

George Parsons Lathrop

The Brotherhood Book of History

'On the North coast of Africa, Carthage is rising. Troy has been sacked. The Sumerian Empire is crumbling. Babylon and Nineveh... In Greece, the Gods of Olympus squabble over the fate of man, whilst in India... A new breed of warrior emerges from the Steppes of Europe...' The first few pages set the scene with broad historical brushstrokes.

I was scanning through the potted history of the world when a word caught my eye on the opposite page: 'Pythagoras'. Given my experiences in the cave, I jumped to it and carried on reading, but with more focus, more attention. I already knew most of what was contained there, and as Thon had said, even the sections I didn't immediately recognise seemed familiar.

Pythagoras was born in the sixth century BC on the island of Samos in the Mediterranean. Under the aegis of his tutor, Pherekydes he was provided with an outstanding education, travelling to Tyre to study with the Chaldeans, to Italy, and to other centres of learning throughout Greece. In his youth he developed an advanced understanding of astronomy, geometry, mathematics and music.

At the age of eighteen, he left Pherekydes and travelled to Miletus to be tutored by the great philosophers, Thales and

Anaximander. There he witnessed the formalisation of classical metaphysics – the conceptual forerunner of the empirical scientific method: What is the cosmos composed of? Is the world all water in differing forms? Is the fundamental substance actually air, denser in some forms, more rarefied in others? What heavenly forces drive the celestial spheres through the ether? What is the nature of the soul? He paid careful attention to the debates, listening intently and taking notes. He formulated his own ideas, and when he spoke, his reputation grew. His fame as a philosopher spread quickly throughout the civilised world and rumours circulated regarding the esoteric powers of his mind: it was said by some that he looked deep into the substance of the world and understood its mechanisms more than any other man. They called him *Philosophos* – lover of wisdom. He was deemed mysterious, supernatural.

When he settled in Samos he built the Semicircle under the patronage of Polycrates, a meeting place where public seminars, lectures and debates were held. Politics, mathematics, ethics, natural science and geometry were discussed there, but not all of his theories were divulged to the public. Nearby, there was a cave, where he held clandestine meetings with a handful of selected disciples – the 'Tetractys Ten'.

As the Semicircle established itself as one of the key sites for intellectual and philosophical enquiry, Samos teetered on the verge of conflict. Polycrates diverted all of his resources to increasing the island's military capability. Pythagoras vigorously opposed this course of action, insisting it would encourage war. He fell out of favour and was forced to leave the island after assuring the Tetractys Ten he would return.

He sought out the Persian mystic and astrologer, Zoroaster, and the Chaldean King, Nebuchednezzar. In India he was initiated into the Brahmin-caste spiritual institutions.

Their emphasis on moral truth and spiritual purity made a profound impression, along with the highly refined theories of reincarnation. In Egypt, he studied the advanced arts of astronomy and geometry.

The most important revelation during his travels arose from comparative studies of music. He discovered a unity in the underlying patterns of the theories and philosophies he encountered, a universal theme threading the different myths of music together. Each culture had its own aesthetic sensitivities and modes of expression, but the ideas regarding the origins and purpose of music appeared to be inspired by the same metaphysical notions. He directed his energies towards the study of music.

When he returned to Samos, the island was poised on the brink of war. He reconvened the Tetractys Ten, who became known as the Mathematikoi, and created the Brotherhood around them. Their ranks were swelled by initiates, known as Nomothets. However, only the Mathematikoi participated in the secret meetings in the cave, and only they were entrusted with the core teachings of the Brotherhood.

The Semicircle was reinvigorated by his return, but in Pythagoras' absence, Polycrates had established a tyrannous reign over the island and was continuing to strengthen the arm of the state. Anticipating war, Pythagoras left the island again and this time took the Brotherhood with him.

Despite his reputation, Pythagoras found it difficult to secure patronage in Greece. He eventually found it in the Italian city of Croton, where he built an institution for the Brotherhood. The Mathematikoi continued to meet in secret, disseminating select facets of their theories to the public and to the growing number of Nomothets, many of whom were citizens of Croton.

By this stage the theory of the three classes of music – *musica instrumentalis, musica humana, musica mundana* – was almost fully developed. Pythagoras had experimented with a method of healing by music, applying in practice the hypothesis of resonance between the musical classes, and substantiating the proposed existence of *musica humana*, which the teachings of the Brotherhood explicitly assume. The argument is extremely simple: the human spirit can be uplifted, calmed, excited or incited to anger by the influence of music. The healing work was the principal method by which the finer details of *musica humana* were discovered.

The Brotherhood's understanding of how *musica humana* and *musica instrumentalis* interact led to the formalisation of a set of laws that described the conventional boundaries between music and mere noise. The key to them both was a highly developed and metaphysical concept of fundamental harmony.

When the Greeks of the Golden Age looked out at the world they glimpsed an underlying order and sought to understand and explain the nature of it. In the sky, they saw order of a heavenly kind in the movement of the stars. It was here that Pythagoras found the final strands of his theory of music. He proposed that the patterns of celestial movement are governed by the same laws of harmony that dictate the patterns of *musica instrumentalis* and *musica humana*. The celestial bodies in their movements produce tones, he reasoned, as all objects in their motion create sound. The tones of celestial motion combine to create a chord of divine harmony: *musica mundana*, the music of the spheres. Musicians, Pythagoras maintained, are synonymous with those who gaze into the heavens in contemplation of the divine. Music is a means of communion with the unseen, the ineffable.

His theory of music was intimately connected with his

belief in reincarnation. Like his peers in the east, he held that the soul could exist beyond death and return to Earth with a different appearance, as a different creature, human or otherwise. He believed it was possible to escape the confines of phenomenal form by continued right-action through successive lifetimes; that the circle of endless rebirth could be broken and the soul subsumed into the divine. Through his metaphysical theory of music, he believed he would find the means to facilitate this moment of transcendence. The secret lay in understanding the nature of *musica mundana*, but to know this, it was essential to have a complete understanding of both *musica instrumentalis* and *musica humana*. The key to understanding all three was the concept of fundamental harmony.

Pythagoras divided his time between studying the mechanics of transubstantiation, developing his theories of harmony and finding ways of describing and sharing everything that he had learnt. A breakthrough came when his old teacher, Pherekydes, became ill with a life-threatening fever.

He left Croton, determined to drive out the sickness with the skills he had honed. He fought to keep the old man from death, using his lyre and his voice to sound the chords he considered most conducive to effecting a cure, but life ebbed away regardless. Eventually, he put the instrument aside and stopped chanting. The world faded from his conscious mind 'like a stone passing through water'. This was the moment of epiphany: the moment when it is said he experienced *musica mundana* directly – the moment he glimpsed the patterns of divine natural law; when the fundamental harmonies revealed themselves; the moment he gazed upon the divine essence and understood something true and unchanging.

When his meditations came to an end, Pherekydes lay

dead.

The restrictions governing entry into the inner circle of the Brotherhood were rigorous. Advancement was based on a stringent ethical assessment of character as much as on intelligence, but no preferential treatment was shown with regard to race, creed, gender or birth. The primary disciplines of the school may have been mathematics, geometry and music, but the spirit behind the study was primarily one of ethics. The social and academic behaviour of potential candidates was observed closely for a period of years.

It was common for members of Crotonic society to seek immediate entry into the Brotherhood as Mathematikoi, even in circumstances where admission to the rank of Nomothet had been refused. Individuals of wealth and rank tried to inveigle their way in, exploiting their status to try to circumvent normal procedure. To guard against this, Pythagoras took an increasingly active role in every stage of the vetting procedure. A politician called Cylon requested entry into the Brotherhood, and Pythagoras rejected the application. Cylon began a campaign of whispers, ultimately turning the powerful men of Croton against the Brotherhood. The institution had overstepped the bounds of Pythagoras' ambitions. It had grown too large, and was accruing a political presence that was undermining the principles upon which it was founded. A plan was set in motion to extricate the Mathematikoi from the institutionalised form of the Brotherhood, allowing Cylon and his cronies to assume control of an empty vessel.

Pythagoras summoned the Mathematikoi and instructed them to abandon the city and scatter to the winds. They told their friends and colleagues they were embarking on extended periods of travel, from which they had no intention of returning. The Brotherhood would live on without a centralised community, free from the wrangling of politics and the petty power struggles of high society. They would dissolve into secrecy and disappear.

The symbol of the Tetractys – the triangle of dots that I'd seen so often on my travels – adorned the door of everyone in Croton affiliated with the Brotherhood. Despite explicit instructions from the Mathematikoi, many refused to remove the symbol on a point of democratic principle. One night Cylon led a party of hired thugs through the streets and burned down any building that he suspected of harbouring members of the Brotherhood, including every house that bore the mark of the Tetractys. A few Mathematikoi were killed, but most of the victims were Nomothets and their families.

When Pythagoras passed away a few years later, he did so in an exile from exile, made homeless twice over. The world moved on and the memory of Pythagoras dissolved into myth and error. When one document places him in Egypt, another has him in Croton, or Greece. Diogenes Laertius wrote one of the most authoritative accounts, in which he stated, *'Pythagoras was the name of four men, almost contemporaneous, and living close to each other. One was a native of Croton, a man with a tyrant's leanings; the second was a Phliason, and a trainer of athletes. The third was a native of Zcynthus, the fourth was this, our philosopher. Some also claim the existence of a fifth Pythagoras, a sculptor of Rhegium. Another was a Samian sculptor. Another, an orator of small reputation. Another was a physician, who wrote a treatise on hernias, and essays on Homer. Dionysius tells us of yet another...'*

According to Thon's book, the Mathematikoi deliberately raised a smokescreen over the history and reputation of their 'Master', and were so effective that within a few hundred years, he was known to the world as a mere mathematician, a discoverer of triangles who was obsessed by the archaic power of numbers. After his death they travelled widely, progressing the theories of music and the art of mathematics, and incorporating strands of knowledge from every culture they encountered. In keeping with their Master's beliefs regarding the transubstantiation of souls, their most important function in post-Crotonic times was to track down Pythagoras, to seek out his soul in the mass of humanity and coax his true psyche from the recesses of his new mind. In this way they facilitated the continuation of his work in its fullest sense. As the years unfolded, the challenge of tracking him became more difficult and they were forced to spread their net wide.

When I closed the book my mind was turning through circles. Who was this man? If everything I had read was true, then in the last two thousand years, who had he been? Who and where was he now? Was he drifting in limbo, waiting for a summons from the earth to give him new life. Was he walking among us? Conscious of the fact that Thon might return at any moment, I rose from the floor, opened the door and walked out into the night. I needed to think, to be alone.

The Brotherhood

Lights were coming on in the narrow streets, bars were filling and the rumbling sounds of the world rose in pitch. The air smouldered with the heady tang of frying food. I put my head down and walked alongside the canal, squeezing the book in my left hand, deep in thought.

All of the other history books were wrong! The historians had been misled, hoodwinked by the Mathematikoi, conjurers of red herrings and false truths. Preposterous, yet what if it were true: that few had known the truth about these people at the time, that those who came afterwards had maintained the impeccable silence? Who were the Mathematikoi?

My wanderings led me into the bustle of the night market. I ambled along, oblivious to my surroundings, but eventually had to stop when I reached a dead-end. I looked up and saw hundreds of fat little monks laughing and grinning. They were Zen lunatics, sculpted from ivory, or something similar. The vendor was shouting, asking me to buy. I picked one up, reached into my pocket and dropped some coins into his hand. He was offended by my lack of enthusiasm for the art of haggling, but I didn't care. I turned and left with a Zen lunatic frozen in the act of banging his drum.

Thon was pouring tea. Incense was burning. He carefully

turned over a second cup and filled it. I put the figurine on the floor and sat down.

'Who are they Thon?'

He handed me the tea.

'It's difficult to say. There have been many.'

'Why is it difficult?'

'Whenever there has been a sudden change in the development of music or mathematics, it is likely that a member of the Brotherhood has been involved, but they live in the shadows. It is difficult to know who they are.'

'You must know of some?'

'We are fairly certain about several scientists, Helmholtz in particular, and some musicians like Bach and Beethoven. Then there was a monk called Guido.'

'Guido of Arezzo?'

'Yes, you know of him?'

'Only a little.'

'He was a Benedictine monk who lived in medieval Italy. He invented a language to transcribe music, using characters he called *neumes*. Before this development, musicians had no way of preserving their art; they relied on their own memory and the memory of others. The method worked fine to perpetuate theories and ideas, but such Chinese whispers play havoc with melodies. The invention of notation was an inevitable step, but he was the first to...'

'I thought the Mathematikoi never wrote anything down?'

'They do not write their *secrets* down, but not everything they do is secret. With language comes the ability to conceptualise. Guido paved the way for the great composers. He made the symphony possible. A vital step, and one that could not be held back.'

'So he was part of your "Brotherhood"?'

'Like Pythagoras, he taught, and like Pythagoras he understood the dangers of the world he lived in. He knew who fed him, but also knew that they could easily starve him, or even kill him if he gave them good reason. When he chose the names of the notes – do, re, me, fah, sol – he took the syllables from the lines of a hymn to St. John the Baptist. In English it goes: *O St John that your servants may with relaxed throats sing the wonders of your deeds; take away sin from their unclean lips*. Have you heard that before?'

'Yes, though your translation is different to the one I remember.'

'How did you come across it?'

'I can't remember.'

'Did you read it, or were you told about it?'

'I can't remember.'

'Do you know why *I* am fond of it?'

I shook my head.

'Whenever a singer warms up by walking through the scales, they inadvertently send this prayer to the heavens. They lift their voices in a plea for spiritual assistance, for the purification of their soul. Most have no idea they are doing it! I imagine poor old St John cursing Guido's name for all the sins he has to forgive – he can never rest. But why did Guido choose *those* lines from *that* hymn? Because he was deeply religious? He was a monk after all. But he was also a teacher and a musician. In his era, where better to pursue these interests than in a monastery? His only other option was patronage, which was difficult to come by. And who wielded all the power and influence in Italy? The Church. A gesture such as this would have convinced the authorities that he was on their side, so they would have left him in peace. Perhaps the monastery was his "Semicircle". Perhaps there was a cave somewhere. You see, for a Pythagorean, the perceptions of others do not matter. This is the greatest lesson you can learn from the book. It doesn't matter what society thinks, so long as you are left in peace. For Pythagoreans, this is paramount.'

'But how can you *know* that anyone was a Pythagorean? Surely there were others who studied independently?'

'I'm sure there were, but don't underestimate the scope of our influence... our net spreads wide.'

It was feasible but far-fetched, demanding my faith and trust. I needed more evidence.

'So who else? More recently?'

'They are too numerous...'

'Anyone?'

'Recently... Herman Hesse. Have you read him?'

'Some. Why Hesse?'

'Have you read *The Glass Bead Game?*'

'Yes, a long time ago.'

'Read it again. The academy of *Castalia* is a metaphor for the Brotherhood, and the *Glass Bead Game* itself is a metaphor for our work: fusing strands of disparate knowledge into a seamless whole, pooling the different views from Max's *clever glass windows*. I presume he told you his theories? We think Hesse grew weary of the burden of secrecy. It could be a coincidence. If so, then it's an uncanny one – some passages are very direct.

'You should also realise that most members of the Brotherhood remain anonymous – Master Ch'ien, for example, and the man who gave you the pendant. The history books will never record their names.

'Not all brothers are active in research – most exist simply to perpetuate the Order, passing on information when it is necessary. Not everyone can be like the Master. The Mathematikoi have always known their place.'

'And you?'

'Take me as you find me.'

'And what about your friend in Tibet? Nathalia?'

'My dear friend, Nathalia. She is studying the *Rol-mo Rig-pa*. If the Pythagoreans made their mark there, she will find it. I told you about her to give you an inkling of *musica mundana* without revealing its true name. I didn't want you know about the Brotherhood before you knew about its work. *Musica mundana* – the music of the spheres – is only a name that we give to an idea, but there are other names.

'So why bother translating all the different names if they mean the same thing?'

'That is a poor question, Sebastian. Languages and ideas arise from different circumstances, different times and places, different people with different perspectives of the world. The Greek ideas are not complete, and it would be arrogant to think that. The *Rol-mo Rig-pa* was born out of a very different culture. It is not complete either. But together, the two theories combine. It is foolish to think that we can achieve what we have set out to do without respecting the efforts of others.'

My head was spinning. I was struggling to accept these ideas, and I couldn't remember my questions. That's why I'd blurted out the last one without thinking. I realised it was stupid, but I followed it with an equally stupid one. 'Is it true, Thon? I mean, do you believe it?'

Thon wouldn't have told me things if he didn't believe them. I'd already accepted that a degree of faith was needed and I'd just proclaimed my lack of it. For a few seconds, I waited. It seemed as if he might not respond. He looked at me with an odd expression: sadness, anger, confusion? I lowered my eyes.

I repeated my question: 'Do you *believe* it?'

'What? The History? The existence of the Brotherhood?

The truth about Pythagoras?'

'All of it.'

'Of course I do. But I have studied the other historians too: Plato, Aristotle, Iamblichus, Porphyry, Aristoxenus, Pempelus, Polus, Diogenes Laertius...I have studied them all. The contents of the book you have just read cannot be contested by the works of ancient historians. Their accounts were written seven hundred years after the collapse of the Order – seven hundred years! They contradict each other constantly. One has Pythagoras in Greece, another has him in Egypt, yet another says he's arrived in Croton. There's no sense in condemning this book on the basis of what has been written by others. Do I believe it? The Brotherhood *was* a secretive organisation, it *did* leave Croton to escape the attention of the local politicians, and the historical records *do* change, the reputation of Pythagoras *does* alter through time. You can trace it for yourself if you have the time. The accounts that were written earlier can't be trusted either.'

'Why not?'

'Because the Mathematikoi never wrote anything down! The commentaries that exist probably came from the Semicircle, not the cave. The Semicircle was filled with Nomothets, not Mathematikoi. They didn't know they were not Mathematikoi, so they probably thought they knew what they were talking about. They were ignorant of their ignorance.'

'But this was written down and *you* gave it to me.' I held the book up into the ensuing silence. The Zen lunatic seemed to draw a breath. He desperately wanted to bang his drum.

'I will tell you why this book exists,' Thon continued. 'The world has changed in the last few thousand years. When Pythagoras died, the Mathematikoi scattered to every corner of the globe. There were times when the links that joined us were perilously weak. The risk of losing our history and our purpose drove the Inner Circle to convene and make sure the disintegration of the Order could never happen. What you have read is the product of this meeting, and others like it. The books are closely guarded. They are printed in limited numbers and the content is deliberately concise. I understand your doubt, but after all you have experienced, after all you have seen and felt, do you really not believe it? Think! How can it not be true?'

I cast my mind back to the cave and the visions of fire and flame. How unnerving those visions were in the light of what I had read. And the words that poured from some hidden conduit in my mind after the first experience in the cave? Since leaving the village I had developed the ability to summon the sensation of *musica humana* at will, and not be overwhelmed in the process. I didn't need a prayer bowl, or the cave. It swirled around my sleeping mind like puffs of smoke blown through rays of sunlight. It filtered into my waking mind. It was fast becoming a ubiquitous part of my life. It was with me in the room with Thon, creating a sense of distance between us, as if the sound of his words was fractionally delayed.

'Why are you telling *me* these things?'

He sighed deeply.

'You move towards knowledge with natural ease. You hear *musica humana*. It is a gift. In the days of Pythagoras, initiates lived in silence for years to develop the discipline with which to approach *musica humana*, but for you it comes naturally, quickly. The book is not shown to everyone.'

My mind was full of clouds, but I could still see questions there like patches of blue sky.

'I don't understand,' I muttered. 'Why was I frustrated? Thon, why am I here?'

A faint rasping noise accompanied his response.

'The Comma.'

It meant nothing to me.

'What is it?'

'The Comma is the reason why we must still exist, why our work is still incomplete. What is it? It is a flaw in everything we have achieved, a blemish on our pursuit of perfection. The Comma is the reason why all music we make today is inherently flawed, why the melodies and rhythms of *musica mundana* remain unknown.'

I hadn't expected this.

'Go on.'

'I presume Max showed you his circles?'

'Yes.'

'The circle of fifths?'

'Yes.'

'It is a falsehood, a fudge. There are no circles in music, just unfathomable spirals. You were looking for neat circles but whether you knew it or not, all you found were perplexing spirals. It is bound to be frustrating.'

'I don't understand.'

'The intervals on the circle are supposed to be perfect, natural fifths. Why *perfect?* The answer to that is mathematical and I presume you know it already. Why *natural?* For one thing, every culture that has looked beyond their first note to find others has come across it; nature reveals it to us. If you blow a simple pipe too hard, you will hear an overtone. The note is the natural, perfect fifth. Each interval on the circle is supposed to be one of these perfect fifths. Unfortunately, if you go all the way round the clock face in these perfect intervals, you never reach the note you began with. You never reach the octave. You never close the circle.'

'What do you reach?'

'Different notes. The distance between twelve perfect fifths should equal the distance between seven octaves, but unfortunately, it does not. The intervals don't add up. The notes have different pitches. The difference is called the Pythagorean Comma. The consequence is that you only have one C at your disposal instead of many – only one D, one E, and one F. You could never make a piano if you used the perfect intervals. The keyboard would go on for miles before any note was repeated. Needless to say, you could never make a guitar either.'

'How big is it, the comma?'

'It's tiny, but it's big enough. The human ear finds it disagreeable.'

'So what does it mean?'

'Exactly what I have said: the circle of fifths is actually an infinite spiral with no notes repeating. Octaves and fifths – the two basic building blocks of instrumental harmony – do not work together. They clash and grate. You have a stark choice to make – music composed using one note in endless repetition, or music with no notes the same. Why? Because you can't put them together without making a mess. Virtually every culture on the planet has tried to use the perfect fifths to build scales because they're naturally harmonic, but it just doesn't work.'

'What about other intervals? What if you forget the fifth and focus on something else, like thirds or fourths?'

'It makes no difference. We've been trying to sort the problem out for centuries, but it can't be done. Believe me, we have tried everything. Music cannot be perfected. It can't do the job we ask of it.'

I would have given anything to see the lunatic bang his ivory drum in that instant and stop grinning at me. A wave of frustration was rising in me. 'What about instruments, Thon?

There are octaves and fifths on my guitar. How can that be if what you say is true?'

'Guitars are made out of broken fifths. So are pianos.'

'Broken Fifths?'

'Broken fifths. Hundreds of years after the death of Pythagoras, music changed. People started experimenting with polyphony, playing different notes together at the same time, which most musicians hadn't done before. The Comma made it impossible because of one terrible problem: it prevented musicians changing key.'

'Why?'

'When you make an instrument, you take one string and tune the others to harmonise with the first one, and with each other. If you use perfect fifths (because they make the sweetest sound), you end up with only a few perfect intervals and many more that are grating to the ear. It's bound to happen because you're trying to force spirals into circles; round pegs into square holes. Some of the intervals inevitably suffer and sound unpleasant. If you play in a different key on the same instrument, the unpleasant intervals occur in different parts of the new scale. If they happen to coincide with part of the scale you use a lot, such as the basic major or minor chords, then you simply can't use these chords. They'd howl. There's no way around it.'

'So what did they do? They must have solved the riddle because...'

'They did *not* solve the riddle. They tried hard but they – we – failed. Now we have equal temperament tuning, which is not a solution.'

'Why not?'

'When you temper the scale, you spread the Comma across all of the intervals, making them all identical in size, but shifting them all slightly out of tune. Instead of having drastically bad intervals mixed up with the perfect ones, all of the intervals are slightly bad. They're all inherently out of tune with each other. In order to be able to change key, we've tuned our instruments to dissonance. It wasn't a new idea. The Chinese thought of it long before the Greeks, but they discarded it. Being able to change key was not worth the sacrifice. Aristoxenus suggested it when Pythagoras was alive, but nobody paid any attention. Besides, Pythagoras never saw the value of changing key. It was counter-intuitive to corrupt perfection, regardless of the practical benefits. Eventually, equal temperament was adopted, but not without cost. Today, no interval we play on a fretted instrument is perfect. If you want to know what frustrated you, it is this: your guitar cannot be tuned. If you're a good listener then you will inevitably be frustrated, especially if you haven't heard of the Comma.'

I knew what he meant, and to be honest, part of me was relieved. I had spent enough hours trying to figure out why one chord sounded in tune when another was not, but I couldn't get to grips with the idea that all music is inherently out of tune. It made no sense. The argument was too sophisticated, too clever. To my surprise, I found myself growing suspicious of Thon's words. He must have sensed my reaction.

'It's a strange thing to consider Sebastian, and most people find it repugnant, but it is true. When tempered tuning took over, there were many detractors, many who said it couldn't be done. They said that the dissonance would be too offensive to the ear, that it would render all music unpalatable. The great composers complained that music would be stripped of its ability to express emotion. With Pythagorean perfect tuning, you could transpose a piece into a different key and the entire mood of it would change because the strange intervals would appear in different places. The different musical modes gave rise to different moods. You can't do that anymore because all the keys are the same. They're uniform, robotic.'

'So if it's so bad, how did we end up with it?'

'It's a remarkable thing that I don't fully understand. We collectively lost the ability to hear. We somehow blended it out. For those who can still hear, it's an obvious mess, but for most people, it isn't even noticeable.'

'And that's why I'm here: the Comma?'

'The piano and the guitar will ultimately leave you unfulfilled, which is both a gift and a curse. The theories of music have failed us.'

These last words jarred painfully. I felt anger. It was a reflex reaction, which I registered without comprehension. Thon was watching me closely, with as much confusion etched on his face as I felt. My head was thumping as if there were voices trapped there, yelling to get out.

'The theories of music have failed us.'

I understood what he had told me about the Comma, and the profound philosophical ramifications it must have had on the Brotherhood, but those final words didn't make sense to me. A thousand great melodies roared through my mind, all of them fashioned out of the supposedly broken intervals of modern music. Some had brought me close to tears; others filled me with joy. I knew it was impossible to tune a guitar, I understood that it must have been the source of my frustration. That made sense. Perhaps I would never play one again, but I wasn't saddened by the realisation. I had found a way to avoid the Comma. I had found a way to escape the constraints of my instruments.

'Have you seen the look in people's eyes when you play?

I asked him. Have you seen what your playing does for *you?* Just physically? With your illness. Nothing's failed.'

'It's difficult to carry on building a bridge when you know you haven't enough bricks.'

'What?'

The anger I felt must have leaked into my tone of voice.

Thon said hurriedly, 'Remember what the book said about Pythagoras and his attempt to revive the dying Pherekydes with music. That's where it all began. That's what we're trying to do. That's what we must do with our instruments. But with the Comma breaking everything apart...it's impossible.'

'Of course it's impossible, but that can't be the purpose of our instruments. It makes no sense. This makes no sense.'

'What do you mean?'

My head was still thumping, but now my words were flowing, quickly, intuitively. 'The Comma doesn't matter. Remember your friend's story about God's question. Maybe the Comma is there to wake us up to something else, something that is dormant in us. If two thousand years of study has shown that it can't be got rid of, then we need to look around it. Say, for argument's sake, that the last two thousand years weren't about getting rid of the Comma at all. What other purpose could there be?'

He looked at me, eyes wide, staying silent.

'To open people's eyes to other possibilities, to switch on as many circuits as possible, to make people realise what lies beneath, or within, or around. Great music, whether tempered or not, can offer a glimpse of what is hidden in Ch'ien's cave. The clues to *musica humana* are hidden in the music of instruments. If Pythagoras had half the intellect you say he had, then he must have known this as soon as he discovered the Comma, or at the very least, not long after. Perhaps he knew this when he was at Pherekydes' bedside. What if the Nomothets were given the task of solving the riddle of the Comma, despite there being no solution? It would be an ideal way to watch them, to see how they work, to evaluate their potential, to...'

The significance of my discoveries and the consequences of having read the book suddenly hit me. Before I could follow my thought, Thon spoke again. He obviously didn't understand what was happening, but for the first time, I felt I did. Chaotic swirls of thought were solidifying into recognisable patterns.

'What were you saying?' Thon asked.

'Huh?'

'You stopped in the middle of your sentence. To...?'

'I don't know.'

But I did. I needed time. Thon spoke again, but I didn't catch his words. Through all of the confusion, I was beginning to understand something vital. The triangle of dots flashed before my eyes. I knew what they meant. I knew what they symbolised.

Thon repeated his question.

'What are you thinking?'

'I don't know.'

I felt as if I'd been punched in the stomach, that the whole world had suddenly been winded. But I did know what I was thinking.

'What are you going to do now? Will you help us to carry on the research?'

'I can't do that Thon.'

'Then you will teach, like Ch'ien?'

Averting my eyes, I found I couldn't answer his question. My mouth froze shut as a vast array of thoughts flooded into my mind in a thousand different voices. The Tibetans made eight classes of musical instrument to mimic the sounds of nirvana. The Chinese believed that by constructing music in accord with the cycles of heaven and earth, a divine harmony could become manifest in both the souls of the people and the holism of the state. In India, Spanda practitioners of the yoga of vibration believed that a perception of the divine universal pulse could be achieved through special meditations. Two-and-a-half thousand years ago, Pythagoras sought to bring the harmony of the spheres to the ears of all people. The list goes on. The seeds were planted everywhere, but the petals of the flowers that grew from them are diverse. I was overwhelmed again by a sense of scale. Hundreds of voices muddied the waters of my mind. I was reeling again, so much so that I barely heard the knock at the door. It came again: a light rapping on the wooden door.

Thon raised his head but didn't move. I waited for him to react. We were both surprised by the unexpected sound. It came again, more urgently, then the door opened and a tall, broad-shouldered figure entered. Thon gathered his wits and addressed the intruder.

'Can I help you? Do I know you?'

'My name is Baldur and I'm looking for Sebastian. Are you Sebastian?'

He turned to face me but I couldn't see his eyes.

'Are you Sebastian?'

'Yes.'

'We've been looking for you. You should come with me.'

Thon remained seated on the floor, mouth agape. The intruder loomed over us, waiting for my answer. He was dressed in the robes of a monk. When his eyes left the shadows, I noticed they carried the pinkish light of the sun with them. His hair was blond, as was his short beard. He was out of breath.

'I don't understand. Who are you?'

'My name is Baldur. I've been looking for you for some time. You must come with me.'

'Why?'

'Because you won't find what you're looking for here. I'm sorry, I'm in a hurry. I can explain everything on the way.'

I said nothing. He waited patiently but I was too stunned by what had happened to think clearly, let alone respond.

'If you need to settle things here first, I can leave you the address. You can follow when you're ready, it's not far.'

He turned his attention to Thon, who seemed to have shrunk in the presence of this stranger. Thon looked more lost and confused than I could ever have imagined. Baldur didn't say a word, but gave him what seemed to me to be a look of compassion. Thon did not speak either. I don't know what passed between them in that brief silence, but for Thon it appeared to be profound and deeply unsettling.

Baldur reached into his pocket. He turned and handed me a card, telling me to go to the address as soon as I could. In a whisper he said, 'It is vitally important to us all that you come and listen to what I have to say. Finish your business here then come as soon as you can. Ask for me, Baldur. I'll explain everything. But I must go now.' In a louder voice, he addressed Thon directly for the first time. 'Please, forgive my intrusion, Master Thon. I will not trouble you again. Goodbye to you both.' He turned, and the door slammed shut behind him.

Mathematikoi

Thon stared blankly at the door. I looked at the card I'd been given and saw the triangle of dots in the bottom left-hand corner. The address was unfamiliar. On the other side was another symbol, a pale yellow circular image, like a halo, with smoothed-out triangular shapes inside. I wanted to chase after the monk, but restrained myself. Thon appeared to have aged drastically. His eyes stared into space.

'Thon?'

He stared at the door. A wisp of pink sunlight bled through the gap at the floor.

'Thon! Are you okay?'

'What?'

'Are you okay?'

'I'm sure I know that man. I must have seen him somewhere.' The flat tone of Thon's voice unnerved me. He sat motionless for a few moments then his body shuddered and he fell into a fit of coughing. I moved closer, put my arm around his shoulder and rubbed his back. He drank the now-cold tea, took some deep, wheezy breaths and looked up. I could find no words, so I simply met his gaze and tried not to betray the sorrow I felt. He spoke in short bursts.

'Sebast…' He coughed. 'You should go now.' Another cough.

'No.'

'I'll be okay. I need to play...yes, that's what I should do. You should go... Please, Sebastian.' He managed to speak the next words clearly without coughing. 'I understand. I see clearly. Let me be. Do what you must do. Go!'

'But...'

'There are no buts, Sebastian. Go, and don't think of me.'

He looked at me and I realised he was right. I gathered my belongings and tried to say goodbye. Thon had picked up his guitar and lost himself in playing. As the notes issued forth, his shivering lessened and his breathing eased. The music gave him more comfort than I ever could.

I thanked him. He didn't appear to hear me.

I left.

I walked around Chiang Mai for hours. People spoke to me, but I didn't hear their words. Motorbikes flew by in silence and the street-vendor's noodles fried without the slightest sound of sizzling oil. My ears were numb and the world was flat and voiceless. I walked without thinking, without seeing.

I found myself at the edge of the city. The sun hung heavy over the rice fields and the cicadas were in full voice, punctuating the stillness with an undulating rhythm of clicks and whirrs that awakened my senses. I sat by the edge of a filthy stream and examined the card that Baldur had given me. It was difficult to come to terms with the implications of his sudden arrival. I put the card away and tried to calm the beat of my heart, relaxing my mind and focussing on the melodies of the world around me. They faded almost immediately and another took over, a smattering of sonorous tones that drew all other sounds into it until there was only one note humming in the air. Focussing deeper, the note collapsed, time froze and the rarefying thrill of the music from the cave took hold of me, welling up from deep within and surging through my body and mind. I felt like a bird of prey diving through the wind, like a swarm of atoms racing through the upper atmosphere or a rush of water flowing over the rocks of a riverbed. This was real. It was all real. I shook off my state of repose and headed back into the town, unsure as to what lay ahead.

It took two hours to track down the address on the card. It was an old monastery, squeezed into the infrastructure of the city between a row of houses and an open-fronted motorbike mechanic's shop. I stood outside, loitering like a lost soul on the pavement, unexpectedly struck by a nervous hesitation. The mechanic was cleaning a moped engine while drinking coffee and talking to a group of friends. They were watching me, no doubt entertained by my display of awkwardness. I tried to smile, and they laughed and turned their attention back to the coffee and the dirty engine. I gathered my courage, walked to the monastery door and knocked hard. The door opened slightly and a young boy stared out.

'Sa-waa dee-krap.'
'Sa-waa dee-krap.'
'Is Baldur here?'
'Who are you?'
'Sebastian.'

I gave him the card. He looked at it, then at me, and spoke: 'Come with me.'

'Kawp Khun Krap.'
'K'p.'

He opened the door wide, inviting me in. We walked through a big entrance hall decorated with plants and simple paintings. Soft, relaxing music emanated from speakers in the ceiling. The young boy walked ahead, looking back every few yards as if he were fearful of losing me. We came to three doors. He opened the middle one and asked me to go in. Baldur sat at a table. As soon as I saw him I felt more at ease. There was something about him that invited trust. He greeted me warmly and offered me a seat, telling the boy to fetch some drinks.

'I'm glad you came, Sebastian. You are most welcome. If you understand the situation as well as I suspect you do, then I'm sure you have many questions for me. Hopefully I have as many answers as you have questions. But first I will ask you one. Do you know who we are?'

'Mathematikoi.'

'Indeed.'

'And Thon?'

The boy returned and placed a jug of aromatic water on the table. He remained in the room. Baldur indicated that he should leave, and he did so, though I could see he was reluctant. Part of me wanted him to stay, perhaps to defer the inevitable answer a little longer.

'I think you know the answer to that question.'

'Nomothet.'

'We don't use the word anymore, but yes, he is a Nomothet.'

'He thought he was like you. He thought he was Mathematikoi.'

He must have sensed that I was upset about Thon. 'It might seem unfair, but it is necessary. You read the book?'

'Yes.'

'Then you will recall that the break-up of the original Brotherhood was a messy affair. Many people died so that we could survive. After the purges in Croton, it was our intention to keep numbers small, but that proved unrealistic. Fulfilling our obligations became more difficult. As the population of the world grew, our task became even more so. In medieval times, we faced a crisis. Our research was progressing, but we consistently failed to find The Master over several generations. We had always accepted that we might miss some of his more obscure incarnations, but it became almost impossible to track him down at all. The Master tends to stand out, and he usually gravitates towards us of his own accord, but by then there were simply too many people in the world. Having lost track of him for several centuries, we decided we needed help. We effectively re-commissioned the rank of Nomothet. Information about the Brotherhood was selectively leaked to communities of fertile minds, where the seeds of the teachings could grow and be nurtured. Those who showed genuine affinity for the teachings were encouraged. The book you read was one of the devices employed.'

'And the Comma?'

'The riddle of the Comma was another means.'

'It has no solution.'

'Indeed, but it serves its purpose. It is a test. Some people struggle with it and are overwhelmed. Others see it for what it is. The test is by no means simple: it took us several hundred years to accept that there was no solution. There are thousands of Nomothets now. We have our eyes on every one. Their fundamental role is to track down potential Mathematikoi, and also to help us find The Master. Often they get it wrong, so we stay in the shadows for a while. We only step in when we're convinced there's a good chance someone has advanced beyond the level of Nomothet.'

'So you think I am one of you?'

'I don't know. We'll find out.'

'How?'

'We have tests. They aren't conclusive, but they'll give us a good indication. You'll know before I do, that's how it usually happens.'

'When did you find out about me?'

'I came to Laos to look for you. I knew that you were visiting Ch'ien and I wanted to catch you before you left. I missed you by an hour, perhaps less, and then you were hard to find. I had to wait until you returned to Chiang Mai.'

'You were in a Landrover, a white one.'

'Indeed I was.'

'I avoided you. I ducked into the forest and went back to the cave.'

'Well perhaps it was for the best. What was it like the second time you went in?'

'I saw things.'

'What did you see?'

'Fire, flames, houses burning, people burning, dying. I saw doors with the triangle of dots. Everyone was in pain and I was overwhelmed by a sense of helplessness.'

'Did you live in this vision?'

'I didn't die, but I think I was about to before I came round. Ch'ien's pendant was burning a hole in my thigh.'

He was silent for a few moments. I had the impression that when he sat with his hand stroking his chin and his eyes looking at the end of his nose, he was thinking deeply and clearly. I drank my water, which was scented with unfamiliar herbs, warming and slightly sweet.

'I would like to ask a few questions, if I may,' I said.

He looked at me for a moment without comprehension, then appeared to break out of his reverie. 'By all means.'

'The image on the back of the card, what is it? I've dreamt about the triangle of dots more times than I can remember and I have met others who recognise it. I've seen it on doors and necklaces, but the second image is one I see only in dreams. Sometimes, I catch sight of it when I meditate: a shadow that fades in and out of focus. When I saw it on your card at Thon's, I realised who he really was, and who you were, but I still don't know what it means. What is it?'

'I could tell you what it is and I could tell you what it means, but it would be much better if I showed you. It would make more sense.'

'Then will you show me?'

'Indeed, but I expect recent events have tired you. It must have been difficult to leave your friend just after he discovered the truth about himself. Perhaps you should rest, enjoy our hospitality for a few days.'

I was worn out, but I didn't want sleep; I wanted answers. 'What about the tests?'

'We will carry them out at the same time I answer your question. The two things are linked.'

'I'd like to do the tests and I'd like you to explain the image on the card. I'd like to do them now. Is that possible?'

'Yes. If you're sure you feel up to it.'

'If I find it too tiring, I'll apologise for wasting your time and graciously accept your hospitality, but I'd like to try. I feel fine, and if I don't do it now I'll be restless all day and even more tired tomorrow. I need answers.'

'All right, wait here. I'll fetch you shortly. If you need anything, ask the boy who showed you in. His name is Noi, he will be in the hall. Try to relax and prepare your mind for meditation. I'm pleased to meet you Sebastian, very pleased indeed.'

'Thank you.'

For the first time since my arrival I had time to think. The room was as sparse as the hallway, with only a table, two simple chairs, the jug of water, two glasses, a vase of flowers, a lamp, and an open window high up on the wall. A fly was buzzing frantically near the ceiling, emitting a slightly flat F. I could hear the soft music from the hall if I concentrated, and occasionally the sounds of the city penetrated through the open window, but otherwise it was quiet. I felt absolutely comfortable and at ease with my surroundings, but both curious and anxious about what was coming next. Tests?

I trusted Baldur, but I couldn't help remembering what had happened to Thon. What if the same thing happened with Baldur? How many layers could there be before I came face to face with the true Brotherhood? How would I ever know I had reached the inner core? When Pythagoras shook me by the hand himself? I wondered what the tests would entail and whether I would pass or fail them. If I failed them, then presumably I was not the man that Baldur thought I was. In which case, had I learned too much? How would they deal with that? I knew very little about the mysterious Brotherhood. To distract myself from such thoughts, I considered what had happened to my friend Thon. His bout of coughing the day before had upset me and I wanted to make sure he was okay. How was he feeling now? Was he ashamed of his ignorance? Did he feel foolish, or had a weight been lifted from his shoulders by the revelation that he did not bear the responsibilities of the Mathematikoi? How long had he laboured under the misapprehension of *who* he was? I resolved to go and see him as soon as I could, regardless of how things went in the monastery. Remembering Baldur's words, I tried to stop thinking and quieten my mind. My eyes were closed and my breathing slow when he returned ten minutes later and asked me to go with him. I followed him down a corridor. The same soft music from the hall was echoing along the walls. We walked past several unmarked doors to one at the furthest end of the corridor. I followed Baldur in and a breeze caught the door and slammed it shut behind us.

The Machine

A large leather chair occupied the centre of the floor. The rest of the room was filled with computers and bulky scientific apparatus. The dull humming of electricity filled the air. Baldur invited me to sit in the chair while he made final adjustments. As I did so, I tried to make sense of the dials and knobs. There was a metal stand with a stream of wires coming out of it. To my right, the bank of computers clicked and purred, and to my left there was an array of machines that I couldn't make any sense of. Before I could study them further, Baldur was at my side, reaching for the wires.

'I need to attach these to various points on your head and chest. They will monitor the activity of your mind and body as we perform the tests. It's quite safe.'

I sat, and he fixed them in place. When they were all attached, he returned to the computer and brought across a pair of headphones, which he placed over my ears. After a final check of all the equipment, he told me what I had to do.

'To begin with, we'll do a few simple tasks for the purpose of calibration. You will hear a different tone in each headphone. One will be low frequency and one high. When I begin, they will both be beyond your range of hearing. You should let me know when you first hear them – there's a button under the armrest of the chair to press. Press it again when they both sound the same. They'll be well separated in frequency, so they'll be many octaves apart, but as soon as you hear two notes that are coincident, you should press the button. Is everything clear so far?'

I found the button on the underside of the armrest. 'Yes.'

'Afterwards, they'll become even closer in pitch until the two cross over and the low note will become high and vice-versa, until they are once again out of range of hearing. Press the button when they coincide, and finally when you can no longer hear them. Is that clear? Are you ready?'

'Yes'

'Then we'll begin.'

I did as he said. Baldur studied his monitor and clicked on his mouse. I completed a series of similar tasks. I did not know if I was doing well or not, as I had no idea what 'doing well' entailed. Then he asked me to meditate, to quieten my mind, which I did. After a while I began to hear sounds in the headphones, a strange collection of drones of different pitches. Sometimes they grated on each other and made me feel uncomfortable. Other times, they created gentle harmonies that washed through my mind and had a cleansing, rarefying effect. Sounds appeared to come from great distances in one headphone and passed through my mind into the other headphone, where they petered out to equally great distances. Resonant beats punctuated the landscape of noise. I found myself tracking certain elements and turning away from others, as I naturally filtered the smooth from the harsh, subconsciously engaging with certain tones and rejecting others. The process lasted for at least another fifteen minutes. When the sound stopped, I felt Baldur's hand on my shoulder and opened my eyes.

'You can rest while I reconfigure the equipment.'

'How am I doing?' I asked him jovially. He just smiled

and returned to his computer. I gazed around the room but all I could see was stars. They seemed to be falling. My eyes took a while to adjust, but eventually the flecks of light disappeared and I could see the contents of the room. I asked Baldur about the stars and he told me such visions were normal. My brain felt like a ball of muscle I had been flexing for too long. I tried to ignore about it and focus on the objects around me. A piece of equipment caught my eye: a transparent plate about six inches across, held in a metal bracket with a circular piece of material on top. It might have been wood, but I wasn't sure. The area inside the circle was filled with a thin layer of transparent fluid, possibly water. Beneath the plate, which was several feet off the ground, there was a lamp pointed at its underside, illuminating the fluid. Several feet above the plate, a camera pointed down. Wires emerged from the underside of the plate and led to a cumbersome box of electronics.

'Okay Sebastian, I'm ready.'

'What should I do?'

'I need you to recreate your experience in the cave. It doesn't matter how long it takes and if you need anything to help you along, I'll do my best to provide it. Ch'ien gave you a bowl...'

'I don't need it.'

'Fine, whenever you're ready, you may begin. As I said, there's no hurry.'

I closed my eyes and focussed, running my mind over the same tracks I'd traced a hundred times since that first night in the cave. Within moments I glimpsed it. The awareness that Baldur was standing next to me did nothing to restrict the flow. If anything, it served to heighten the experience. I fell into comfortable repose, surrounded and absorbed by the thrilling rhythms that pervaded my body and soul, floating, diving, rising, rushing, flowing. But then something surprising occurred. The sensation suddenly intensified. An unfamiliar thrill coursed through me. I had a glimpse of something I could barely conceive of: universal, massive. My heart raced and a surge of excitement interfered with my thoughts, pulling me away. I opened my eyes. Pins and needles struck the skin of my arms and face as I heaved in a gulp of air. I felt as if I hadn't taken a breath for an hour. Baldur was leaning over me, staring intently. His eyes darted to the computer, back to me and to the computer again. Then he moved to the keyboard and began to tap on it. I stood up and shook my hands as if they were wet, making slapping noises with my tongue and swallowing compulsively. An electrical charge was jolting me. I thought for a moment that I had been electrocuted.

'That never happened before,' I said between swallows.

'What was it?'

'I don't know. I've never felt anything like it.'

'Did it hurt you?' He sounded concerned.

'No. Not when it was happening, but I feel awful now. I panicked because I wasn't expecting it, but it wasn't painful. My body panicked. If I could control it more... I could try again.'

'No, Sebastian. You should rest.'

'What do your machines say?'

'They don't understand.'

'What should they understand? What are they for? What do they do?'

'The test measures the intensity of the *second repetition*, detecting and amplifying the fingerprint of it in your cognitive...'

'Wait! The second repetition? What?'

'Drink this.'

He handed me a glass of water. I drank it in one. He refilled it from a jug. I drank that and filled it again myself.

'What is it?'

'Come here and I'll show you. I'll answer your question about the card at the same time.'

He took me over to the machine and flicked some switches. The water immediately began to move. He told me that the plate was made to vibrate by passing an electric current through a set of crystal vibrators attached to the underside. The vibrations passed from the plate to the fluid. At specific frequencies, standing wave patterns emerged in the fluid and could be seen through the camera. He adjusted a dial and told me to look at the screen. I saw a set of concentric circles in the surface of the water, as if a stone had been cast into a pond and the ensuing ripples frozen. He told me to keep watching as he increased the frequency. The circles began to lose their integrity, quivering slightly, then breaking apart in tiny explosions. The surface became chaotic, boiling and popping like a hot cauldron.

After a short while, as Baldur continued to increase the frequency, the water reorganised itself into another pattern. The change wasn't gradual. On the contrary, first there was definite order, then utter chaos, then order again. The new pattern was more complex, like a snowflake. Baldur increased the frequency again and the pattern subsided again into chaos. He continued to turn the dial, and eventually another pattern emerged, yet more complex. Each time a new pattern formed, it displayed more symmetry, more intricacy, and was more beautiful.

'The vibrations you pass through the plate impose structures on the water.'

'Indeed. There are certain harmonic frequencies that the fluid responds to, and it spontaneously organises itself from chaos when you expose it to them. At all other frequencies, the vibrations are chaotic. You have to look beyond the plate and the water to understand what this means. The whole universe is in a perpetual state of vibration, from the smallest speck of matter to the most massive bodies we know of. Everything moves and everything vibrates. Electrons spinning around atoms exhibit the same behaviour – they will only order themselves at specific energies, hence the *quantum* in quantum physics.'

'Everything moves and everything vibrates.'

'Indeed. On an even lower level, you have the *strings* of string theory.'

'So, what sets them all in motion? If the universe is the water on the plate, what are the crystal vibrators?'

'Given what I've said so far, that is the perfect question. You're talking about an original sound, a primordial boom that triggers the universe and sets everything into motion.'

'The big bang?'

'You could call it that. We know that sound imposes structure on matter – you've seen it on the plate with your own eyes. At the right frequency of vibration, could the tiniest specks of matter be driven into increasing levels of complexity? Perhaps subatomic particles could be driven to adopt the more complex structures we call atomic particles. Perhaps atomic particles could be driven to reorganise into even more complex structures by the presence of other frequencies and form molecules. The logic proceeds all the way to stars and galaxies, and to life itself. I look in a microscope and see landscapes that are identical to the ones I see with my unassisted eyes. I stare through telescopes and see the same patterns as I see in a grain of sand. Harmony is the guiding principle behind the construction of matter. The physical universe is a harmonic structure. Sound is the fundamental organising principle of everything we see and feel.'

'You mean like the Hindu *Aum*.'

'Indeed – the fundamental harmony, the creative principle, the complex chord of notes that gave voice to the big bang, the sound that begat the universe and gives form and structure to everything in it.'

'Incredible.'

'And we've found clear evidence of it.'

'What?'

'The whole universe still reverberates with the primordial voicing of its creation. We've found traces of it in the cosmic background radiation, the so-called 'aftershock' of the big bang – the echo of the Aumic boom.'

'But we can't hear it?'

'It's well below the range of our ears. It's loud though, just impossible to hear. It's always there, reverberating in every single pore of the universe.'

I stepped back from the screen and collapsed in the chair. He removed the plate from the machine and carefully inserted another in its place. Then he turned to me and waited. I had found everything he said entirely reasonable. Though I had never trained as a scientist, I could grasp principles and theories with relative ease. Nothing struck me as irrational or implausible. When I looked up, he beckoned me to return to the plate, which he had removed and replaced with another.

'I haven't yet answered your question, and there is more to see. The machine can be modified to accept amplifications of naturally occurring sounds, such as speech or bird song, or chanting – anything really. I've got a recording that I'm going to feed into the vibrators. Look at the screen.'

'Why did you change the plate?'

'I replaced the water with oil. It responds better for this frequency range. Now look and tell me what you see.'

'What is the recording?'
'It's a chant.'
'Aum?'
'Indeed. You're ahead of the game.'

I looked at the screen and saw the oil shimmering, as if in anticipation. Then the recording began, the crystals vibrated and the oil spontaneously arranged itself into a pattern, an image I recognised: the image from the card, identical in every way to the image from my dreams.

'Aum,' I whispered quietly to myself.

'Aum,' Baldur repeated.

We stood over the plate and watched the rippling contours of the fluid until a question sprang to my mind.

'The second repetition? What did you mean by that?'

'According to the Hindu tradition, there are three *repetitions* of Aum. The first is the chanted form, the audible intonation of the syllables that you hear in monasteries. The second is said to occur when the lips move but no sound is heard. It's a reflexive and contemplative form that can be used to alter the patterns of your brain function and influence the timbre of your spirit. The third is inaudible and mysterious. It is said to be sensed in deep meditation. It is the highest repetition.'

'*Musica instrumentalis; musica humana; musica mundana* – the highest repetition: the music of the spheres.'

'Indeed.'

'And the *Rol-mo Rig-pa* too.'

'The very same.'

'The tests... you were "listening" to the second repetition, to *musica humana*, to the music of the cave.'

'Indeed.'

'How?'

'We found the traces by watching the way our brains behave when it is occurring. The machine analyses the frequencies of your brainwave function, mostly in the temporal lobes. It's quite straightforward.'

'Could you record the output and amplify it.'

'I suppose we could.'

'Could you direct the amplified signal into this machine? Could you send it to the plate?'

Baldur brought his hand to his chin in a swift and direct movement, raising an eyebrow and shaking his head slowly with thought. 'I suppose we could. I'm ashamed to say it, but we've never thought of it.'

'I think we should do it.'

'I think you're right.'

'When can you begin?'

'I'll start making the changes immediately. If all goes well I should have it done by tomorrow, though there may be problems I haven't yet anticipated. I'll need to think it through. But now, you need to rest Sebastian.'

'I think you're right. Is there somewhere I can be alone? Somewhere quiet where I won't be disturbed? I need to think, and sleep.'

'Indeed. Come with me.'

I followed him back down the corridor to the entrance hall. Noi was sitting in the corner reading a book. He leapt to attention as soon as we entered. Baldur gave him instructions, then bowed his head, wished me well and headed back to the machine room to make the alterations to the equipment. Noi smiled widely with glowing eyes and half walked, half skipped down another corridor. I was surprised how heavy and tired I suddenly felt, but his excitement lent me additional energy I needed to reach my bed. I fell into it and when my head hit the pillow I slept instantly. On that evening, my mind, body and soul were utterly exhausted.

The Earth Moves

I'm sitting in absolute darkness, naked. The air is cool and wet. Water is dripping, slapping against the floor. I'm deep in the heart of a huge mountain, smothered in rock. Tremendous weight hangs above me. A stupendous tribal drumming emanates from deep below, as if the mantle of the earth is being pounded. The underworld shudders. The forces penetrate the flesh of the earth, pass through the cave, through the mountain out into the sky and further, beyond the atmosphere, permeating the ether in every direction for thousands of miles. The vast emptiness of space swallows it. The cave rumbles.

I place my hands on the floor. The rough grooves of the earth press on my soft fingertips. It is cold. I close my eyes, and am blinded by light. When I open them, it is pitch black. When I close them, the light returns. With closed eyes, I watch it fade from blinding white to radiant, deep amber. The shape of a man appears, but the light is too bright to see him clearly. I try hard to distinguish his face. I try to speak, but my mouth does not respond. I'm sure I've seen this face before, in mirrors, in water, always distant, veiled by shadow or bleached by light.

A strong wind blows. The figure reaches out with fiery arms. I stretch out my own arms. The wind blows. Our hands connect and we are lifted from the ground, spinning like flotsam in a whirlpool. A terrifying maelstrom engulfs the cave. The temperature soars, ripping apart the bonds that hold the rock together, melting the walls as if they were butter. Our bodies strain against immense pressures. An almighty scream erupts from my soul and every fibre of my being tenses against the inevitable. My flesh falls away. My bones split asunder. The walls are torn apart. More light enters the cave. The air simmers and boils. My flesh has gone. My bones have gone. I am energy, swirling. He is energy, swirling with me. We are plasma.

An almighty explosion tears the fabric of space and obliterates the mountain peak. The summit falls, crashing to the ground which swallows it up and sucks it into the belly of the earth. Dust, smoke, plumes of ash are rising, atomised by the heat. The stars appear. The unending vista of the universe extends, cooling the inferno like a cosmic heat sink, sucking in its rage and silencing its fury. Gradually, it settles.

I am on my knees, a spirit dressed in flesh and bone. The figure I saw is bound to me. We are fused. Aftershocks ripple through the earth like rushes of ecstasy. My thoughts are lucid, my skin is cool and I am alert. The rumbling of the earth tells me something. It tells me I must remember. I must remember the event. It is coming, but I must remember. I must rem...

I woke up by the side of the bed on my knees, gasping for air, my hands pressed firmly against the cold floor, arms shaking, sweat pouring from me. The floor felt as though it was moving, but I was nauseous and disorientated. The whole world was spinning. What time was it? I had no idea. How long had I slept? I lifted myself off the floor and got back into the bed, shivering, although it wasn't cold. The air tasted like fresh water. The light was hazy. My skin was tingling. None of these observations explained a fundamental feeling of difference in the world. But the change wasn't just in the world, it was inside me. I was different, my mind was quiet. There were no voices apart from my own, no unbidden questions, no chaotic swirls of thought or idle chatter, no noise. The clatter had gone.

I must remember. That was the last thought I'd had before I awoke. I sensed a gap where the forgotten memory should have been. I sat up in the bed, crossed my legs, closed my eyes and revelled for a few moments in my internal silence. The sensations of the cave welled up naturally. It was like moving an arm, turning my head or breathing. Tides of sweet harmony engulfed me. I sat absolutely still, but I was spiralling, stretching in every direction, my form blurring, spreading out, rarefying. Air was passing through me.

The experience intensified. An ineffable sense of unity suggested itself as if from a great distance, then crept closer. A sense of overwhelming massiveness pervaded my mind, coupled with a feeling of being in contact with every other fragment of matter. The first wave of this sensation knocked me breathless, and my body heaved a great gulp of air from the world. There were no sounds, no notes, no tones, no structure, no beats, no melody to speak of. After the first wave, I recoiled instinctively. When the second wave arrived – more intense than the first – I leapt backwards as if I'd been struck physically. My heart was burning and my lungs were rasping. I was shaking, murmuring uncontrollably.

It took me a while to recover, but as soon as I was able, I stood up, dressed and went to find Baldur. He was talking to Noi in the entrance hall. They stared intently. I was breathing hard and sweating profusely.

'Baldur, how long have I been sleeping?'
'A night and a day. It is early evening.'
'Is it ready?'
'It is.'
'Then we must begin.'

I headed towards the machine room. He had no choice but to follow. When I entered the laboratory, I noticed that the chair had been moved closer to the plate.

Baldur started flicking switches. 'I've set it up so we can record the behaviour of the fluid. If anything happens, you'll be able to view it afterwards.' He moved towards me. 'I need to attach the wires as before.' He continued to talk as he did so. 'The signal will be amplified to a sufficient level to exert an influence on the fluid, but I'll be able to monitor and adjust the intensity as the experiment proceeds. If it goes to plan, we'll see the shape of your mind, so to speak. Are you ready? Are you sure you don't need something to eat or drink, you've been asleep for a long time.'

'I'm fine Baldur. Please – attach the wires and we'll begin.'

He adjusted the instruments as I tried to slow my heartbeat and relax my traumatised body. When he was ready, I rubbed my face with my hands, gathered my composure, closed my eyes and focussed. The second repetition flooded through me without effort. I could barely control the surges; they came unbidden. I opened my eyes. Baldur sat watching the equipment with his back to me. Without removing the wires from my head, I got up and put my hand on his shoulder.

'Well Baldur, what did you see?'

I think I surprised him, he turned suddenly.

'You can see it for yourself. It's still there.'

He pointed to the plate, and I saw exactly what I had expected to see: the shape of the symbol from the card; the shape of the chanted Aum – except the peaks were higher, the troughs were lower and the pattern persisted even though I was no longer in meditation and no signal was being sent to the plates.

'Why does it persist?' I asked, but he didn't answer. We stood watching for a few more seconds, then suddenly it fell apart. 'What happened? What else did you see?'

'Several patterns formed as you went into trance. Each of them broke down. A period of chaos ensued before the next one formed. It settled on the one you just saw.'

'What do you think?'

'It's a revelation. It's unforgivable we haven't thought of it before.'

'It's not important, Baldur. We have more to do.'

'What do you mean?'

'Something happened when I was sleeping. I think I know what, but I'm not sure yet. Perhaps nothing will happen, but I want to try. I am waking up, Baldur.'

'I know.'

'Then let's do this. Reset the equipment, exactly the same as before.'

'Indeed.'

I went back to the chair and waited for Baldur to give the go-ahead. When he did so, I repeated the same procedure as before, but this time I let the floodgates open. For a while, nothing happened. Then my skin began to crawl. Jets of electricity ran down my arms and across my chest. Once again the sense of overwhelming massiveness pervaded me and I was consumed. My hands touched stars and carved an arc through time. Light danced around me in every colour there could ever be. I was hurtling, roaring, rarefied in a billion tiny intervals of sound. I heard a pop and a tiny explosion from far away, two sounds that were completely incongruous at the time. They disturbed me. The tingling of my body had long since ebbed away and I was physically numb, but far beneath me I suddenly sensed my body, seated motionless in the chair and covered in wires. It was suffering, even though

I could barely feel its pain. My heartbeat was like a distant metronome marking out a sluggish time and tying me to my skin. I could feel my lungs struggling to draw in air, and I lost concentration completely. The lights blurred to grey. I crashed back into my body and agony coursed through me like nothing I had experienced before. The contrast in the few moments that marked either side of the transition couldn't have been more intense. I tried to howl, but there was no air in my lungs; I hadn't been breathing. My heart was palpitating wildly, missing beats then beating furiously at awkward intervals as if to compensate. My bones ached, my skin crawled and it felt as though a vice were relentlessly closing on my head. Blood pulsed against the back of my eyes. My eardrums were burning, ringing, throbbing.

Baldur was leaning over me, mopping my brow with a wet cloth and shouting my name – or somebody else's. He stopped when I took hold of his shoulders with both hands and he pressed his forehead against mine. My heart was still racing and my body twitched with each misplaced beat, rushes of blood heaving into my brain in confused pulses. The lack of control edged me towards panic, but the pain gradually subsided and my body managed to regain its natural rhythms.

I noticed a puddle of fluid spreading on the floor. There were tiny fragments of glass everywhere. Flecks of it glinted on Baldur's arms and specks of blood were spattered on his right cheek and temple. When I recovered my composure, I pulled away from Baldur and asked, 'What did you see?'

Baldur answered me directly. He told me exactly what I needed to know, as he had done on every occasion since our meeting. He was a scientist, a pragmatist, a clinician, a consummate Mathematikoi. 'I saw the Aum pattern form when you went into the second repetition, just as before. It didn't disappear and reform into another pattern. It grew more rigid, more defined, but the water tension made it tremor and vibrate. I looked up and you were shaking violently. I put my hand on your forehead. It was burning. Your temperature soared, but there was nothing I could do. I shouted your name but you couldn't hear me. Your eyes rolled back into your skull. Your face was drawn and taut, like the water. I went back to the apparatus to see what was happening, but before I got there, the plate blew apart, breaking into tiny shards.'

'Are you okay?'

'They hit the side of my face and my arms, but the injuries are superficial. I'm fine.'

'Something is missing. Something isn't right. There shouldn't be so much pain. Do you know what the *event* is, Baldur?'

'Which event?'

'Of course you don't because I never told you. I should have. I should have told you, but you weren't there. I couldn't find you.'

'Told me what?'

'Something is going to happen, I'm sure of it, and I need to know where and when. I should have waited when I saw your Landrover in Laos. I should have arrived here sooner, but how was I to know? I slept too long and now we are in a race against time, Baldur. I feel it. Either time is moving too fast or I am moving too slow. We need to act quickly.'

'What should I do?'

'Take me back to my room and call the Mathematikoi. Summon them all. Maybe one of them will solve the riddle. I need to rest. I need to rest, and maybe to dream.'

Since the first fevered vision in London, I had learned to

trust my dreams. So often they had guided me when I was lost. They had led me out of a long, deep sleep, but my intuition told me that they could tell me no more. The voices were silent, and there were no more images to decode. I had no dreams that night. I had awoken.

Baldur led me to my room, laid me on the bed and left to issue the summons to the Mathematikoi.

The Master had returned.

Thon

Noi was standing at the side of my bed, tugging at the sheet and speaking my name. I lifted myself onto one arm and stared with half-closed eyes as he told me in a whisper that Thon was not well. I didn't take it in. I thought he was an apparition, a dream. I asked him to repeat his words, and he did so in triplets: 'Baldur sent me. Thon is ill. He might die.'

'Then I must go to him.'

'Baldur said you'd say that. He told me to bring you tea and make sure you ate this food.' He pointed to the bedside table. 'You aren't allowed to leave until you've eaten. Baldur said so.'

'Did he *indeed?*'

'*Indeed* he did.'

His expression lit up with the mischief of my light-hearted mockery and I found myself giggling with him. The news about Thon was still surreal. I followed Noi's instructions and ate the food, though I didn't feel hungry. The tea was revitalizing and my thirst was unquenchable. While I ate and drank, Noi sat on the end of the bed and scrutinized my every move, as if he expected me to hide the food and say I'd eaten it. It was quite clear he wasn't going to let me go anywhere until I had cleared my plate.

'Tell me Noi, how do you come to know Baldur?'

I had jumped to the conclusion they were not father and son because one had Scandinavian features, the other Thai.

'He's my father,' he said, clearly surprised.

'I beg your pardon, Noi. I didn't know.'

'People don't guess, but it's true. He says my mother made the decisions and that's why I look like her and not him. She's dead now, but she still talks to my father. He says when I grow up and I'm old, I'll be able to hear her too. He says you can hear her everywhere when you're older – if you learn to listen. He's teaching me to listen.'

'And every day you grow up a little bit more.'

'And every day I listen.'

'Then one day you will hear.'

'Maybe.'

His face was etched with pride, love and the longing of youth.

'Do you live here all the time, Noi? Is this your home?'

'We move around a lot. We have homes in Thailand, and Laos and Kampuchea and China and Burma and Vietnam. My father has to move around because he needs to see lots of different people. People like you, except you're different. He likes you.'

'Well I like him too, Noi. *Indeed* I do.'

He chuckled again but hid his face from me, no doubt ashamed for laughing at his father's expense, albeit in an innocent way. When the food was consumed and the teapot drained, Noi cleared away the debris and ceremoniously informed me I was free to leave whenever I wanted to. I thanked him with an equal attention to ceremony and got dressed.

Baldur greeted me in the entrance hall and told me that the call had been put out and the Mathematikoi were on their way. I thanked him, and asked him about Thon's condition. He hadn't been able to attend to my stricken friend personally, but he made it clear that the situation was grave. Thon had refused medical treatment and was dying.

I said goodbye and left.

When I arrived at Thon's home, a young monk was sitting beside him. He rose when I entered, placed a wet cloth in a bowl on the floor, bowed and left. I approached the bed and was horrified by Thon's appearance, amazed how quickly his health had deteriorated in the few days since we had last seen each other. Thinking over the time I had known him, I suppose it was inevitable that the worst would happen sooner rather than later. He had good spells and bad, but over time his health had never significantly improved. He hung on precariously. I felt an aching sadness when I saw him lying on the bed, shaking with fever. The air was thick and muggy and saturated by a foul smell, the acrid breeze that always blows before death comes. I lit several sticks of incense then went to his side.

'Thon. Thon, it's Sebastian.'

His eyes rolled deliriously and he struggled to focus on my face. The fever was taking control and he was ominously weak and distant, like a shadow cast in twilight.

'Who? It's you? I found you? *I* found *you.* Hold my hand and tell me? *I found you.*'

'You found me, Thon.'

'I did. Even though I wasn't right. I found you. You will see the lake. You will see the water and you will swim, and, the water, so cold…'

His voice trailed off and he fell into a violent fit of coughing. The sound of it was horrifyingly abrasive and penetrating. I felt great pity but was simultaneously plagued by helplessness and frustration at my own inability to rescue him from his fate. What could I do to ease the turmoil that he endured as his body failed him? His eyes were wild and his veins were standing out. He retched uncontrollably but failed to bring anything out of his exasperated lungs. He was empty of life, but his body was not finished with him. It was holding on. When the attack finally subsided, his body was so weak he couldn't lift his arms. He shook like a frost-bitten child, and his breath came in hoarse gasps. He looked up with unfocussed eyes as I returned his head to the pillow with all the care I could, and then – for a few moments – he seemed to see me clearly. His lips formed words. I leaned closer, put my ear next to his mouth and listened as he spoke in a barely audible, yet entirely coherent whisper.

'Sebastian', he said, '*I cannot play.*'

I lifted my head and his eyes were filled with unimaginable sadness and pain. His eyes were staring deep into mine, searching for a glimmer of hope. A tear left my eye. By the time it rolled off my cheek and fell onto his face, the moment of clarity had gone and his eyes were rolling without comprehension, lost in a delirium that he would never break free of again. I held his head in my arms and wept. His dying words never left me, and at the time they struck me like a blow from a fist: *I cannot play*, which meant: 'I am dying.'

His guitar was on the floor. I picked it up and played for him. I had done this once before, wrongly believing I could save someone by simply plucking the strings. It was not possible to turn off time and end decay by composing chords, but it was possible to alleviate the pain and replace it with warmth. The change was noticeable immediately.

In the early evening, Baldur came in with two other monks I had never seen before. His face paled when he saw how ill Thon was, but he quickly gathered his composure and attended him with the same gentle strokes of a wet cloth that had soothed me so well in the monastery the night before. After a short while, he stood up and returned to his colleagues, who were standing in respectful silence. They began a low chant that must have lasted for nearly an hour. It fell naturally into the spaces around the notes I played. Baldur and I did not converse during his visit. As he left, we bowed to each other, and I was alone with Thon once more.

Several hours later, three strangers arrived. They were dressed in the ceremonial clothes of Hmong tribesmen. I didn't stop playing, but acknowledged them with a nod of my head. I think they were initially confused by my presence, but after a moment of hesitation, they bowed respectfully and sat down next to me on the floor. Unwrapping yellow cloths, each took out a gold necklace and placed it round his neck, speaking in whispers that I could barely hear. From larger packages they took out mouth organs made of wood and bamboo. They listened closely for a few moments then joined in. We played until the last shiver subsided and Thon's body lay calm and still on the bed. I stopped, but the others continued. According to their rituals, the *Khaen* pipe should be played for several days after the death of a loved one. They believe that the harmonies create a bridge to the world of their ancestors. Without the ceremonial playing of the *Khaen*, the soul of the dead would be trapped like a spectre in the world of the living, unable to touch or feel anything, disconnected from their ancestors for eternity. I held Thon's hand for a moment, looked at his face for the last time and left without saying a word. He looked serene. All the pain had gone. My heart was sad, but I was glad his suffering had come to an end.

A dry wind blew down the road and rustled the leaves of nearby bamboo grass. Hundreds and thousands of stars filled the sky. The air was warm for the season. A day and a half had passed, and I still didn't have an answer to the riddle of my dreams. At the monastery, the Mathematikoi were convening.

I walked through Chiang Mai in a daze. My reserves of energy had been consumed by the unrelenting intensity of the past week, and I realised I would have to go straight to bed when I returned to the monastery. I craved a pause, a few hours in which to reflect and watch the world pass by without concerns and confusions. Taking a circuitous route back to the monastery, I wandered past places steeped in memory.

As I walked past a familiar cafe, the owner called out and ushered me to a table by the roadside, the same table I had always chosen. He brought me the same drink: sweet Indian chai. We talked for a while then he left to serve another customer. I sipped the aromatic tea and paid idle attention to the life drifting by. I listened to the sounds of the world: the sizzle of a *pad thai* noodle fryer in the street; the incessant drone of the motorbikes; the rhythmic slapping of flip-flops on tarmac; the melodic pitter-patter of Thai being spoken around me; the slurp of the chai as it passed my lips; the beats of my heart like dull and distant rumbles. Every individual element was a distinct melodic line. The world was an endless symphony. I remembered the first time I had realised there was mystery in music. I was a young child, sitting on a rock beneath a waterfall in a forest in rural England. Three separate plumes of water cascaded past, one on each side and one directly in front of me. I was watching intently, fascinated by the perpetual movement and the glint of the sunlight dancing in the white water. When I closed my eyes and listened, I realised I was hearing a chord. The three plumes of water produced distinct musical notes as they crashed on the rocks. I sat for a long time, switching my attention from one to the other. I experienced a feeling of nostalgia that I couldn't comprehend, but which filled me with an overwhelming sense of wonder How can you yearn for something when you do not know what it is?

That night I asked my parents for an instrument, any instrument. They bought me an acoustic guitar. The memory was a fond one, but it was just one of many. How often had I discovered music for the first time? How many times had I known the pleasure of discovering the world speaking in tones? How many more times would I have to discover it again before I understood it? I drained the teacup, thanked the owner with a promise to return and headed directly back to the monastery. I never kept that promise.

The Event

Noi opened the door and the sound of voices flooded out. He smiled and stepped aside. The entrance hall was filled with people, who stopped talking as I entered and turned towards me, staring. I stared back with a vague sense of recognition. I didn't recognise their faces, but every time I met someone's eye, I felt bonded, familiar. I was looking at the Mathematikoi. They stood with confidence and authority, exuding calm composure. Their collective intelligence seemed to charge the air. For a few moments the ambient music that drifted down from the ceiling was the only sound in the room. I felt some strength returning, and I found myself smiling. Baldur – no doubt noticing how shaky my legs were – stepped from the group and took my arm. I thanked him and greeted the newcomers briefly, apologising for my fatigue and assuring them we would meet again when I had rested. Baldur moved me quickly through the gathering and into the haven of my bedroom, then left me. Once again, I slept for a day and a half.

When I awoke, I found that the rest of the Mathematikoi had arrived in a buzz of expectation. My arrival, the innovation with the machine, and the implications of the experiment that Baldur and I had conducted combined to generate an atmosphere of anticipation. Baldur had repeated the experiment himself whilst I was attending Thon. He'd seen the familiar shape materialise on the plate as he'd entered the second repetition, and the contours had remained for a few seconds after the end of his meditations, but the plate had stayed intact. The rest of the Mathematikoi were eager to have their turn.

Something else happened while I slept. I had no discrete dreams, but in my subconscious repose I passed in and out of more memories than I thought it possible to have. I relived every revelation, every reawakening. I recalled the construction of symphonies, the reinvention of ancient languages, the struggles that gave birth to great leaps of scientific understanding, countless objects of my affection, thousands of familiar landscapes, the appalling shock of birth and the excruciating anguish of death. I saw myself stretched thinly over timescales that were mind-boggling. Sebastian was a name by which my family and friends had known me. With the sudden influx of so many other memories, I found I could barely remember him and his family. The Mathematikoi were my true family. They always had been. My kinship with them was unbreakable. I awoke with my new memories dancing through my mind. I lay on the bed staring at the ceiling and trying to put them in order, but the task was too great and I turned my mind to the most important thing that still remained for me to do – *I must remember the event*. It was the last puzzle left to me, an empty space in my mind where I knew something should fit. I searched through my subconscious but I couldn't find an answer. I thought of Thon. On his deathbed he'd said something that hadn't made sense. I'd let it pass because he was delirious with pain and I didn't want to sully his final moments with an interrogation: 'You will see the lake. You will see the water and you will swim...'

What had he meant? If it was relevant, how could he know when Baldur and the Mathematikoi did not? I considered everything that had happened in the last week and tried to isolate those things I hadn't understood, seeking anything that might give me a clue. I remembered waking up from the dream with my hands on the cold floor, convinced the earth was rumbling beneath me. Had I still been dreaming when it happened? Or was it just nausea?

I got out of bed, knelt down and placed my hands on the floor. It was still cold, but it definitely wasn't moving. I lowered my head and placed my ear to the ground, trusting in fate to spare me an interruption and the subsequent need to explain my strange prostration. I heard nothing, but I stayed there, kneeling on the floor. Then I sensed something: a shudder. Was I imagining it? I remained still and listened intently, drifting deeper into the second repetition as I did so. I felt it again, a movement that began at my fingertips and spread up my arms to the base of my skull. I focussed harder.

Without warning, a silent blast knocked me backwards, a sudden jolt that seemed to push me up from the ground. I was stunned. I wasn't dreaming. I remembered what Baldur had said: *Sound is the fundamental organising principle of everything we see and feel...Aum...the fundamental harmony, the creative principle, the complex chord of notes that gave voice to the big bang, the sound that begat the universe and gives form and structure to everything in it.* The voice of God. The Tao. In the beginning there was the Word and the Word was...*well below the range of our ears...loud though, just impossible to hear... always there, reverberating in every single pore of the universe.*

Wherever matter accumulates in the vast, empty universe, the residual echo is felt more keenly, concentrated in the accumulations; matter is congealed sound. Every celestial body is a concentration of tones, a complex combination of interrelated harmonic structures. The primordial sound drives the subatomic particles to adopt harmonic structures: atomic particles, molecules, organisms, planets and stars – life itself. The Earth resonates with it, from every one of its elementary particles, to every desert, mountain, river, lake or ocean. It binds them, forging them from a swirl of chaotic energy, just as the fluid on the plate is given structure by the vibration of the crystals. The entire Earth is like the fluid on the plate, and the signal that puts it together piece by piece is the elusive Aum of Indian myth: *musica mundana* – the music of the spheres.

I returned to the floor and slipped into meditation, focusing my efforts into repeating the experience that had shattered the plate. I knew beyond doubt what it was – a glimpse of the third repetition, of the elusive *musica mundana*. It was dangerous to practise alone because it proved impossible to gauge time when I was ensconced in it. I was oblivious to the strain on my body. As I passed through the familiar *musica humana*, I tried to resist the numbing effect on my body, forcing myself to maintain the connection so that I could interpret the sensations in the palms of my hands as they began to tremble. The effort was immense, and I struggled to control it. The Earth was alive with noise: an immeasurable grinding of vast tectonic plates; huge pressures locked together in a precarious tension. The deep rumbling shook the palms of my hands. The very core of the Earth was roaring with urgency. It was restless.

I couldn't maintain concentration. I came crashing back through the repetitions and found myself lying on the floor, gasping for air, my heart wild with panic and my skin quivering. I couldn't keep doing this.

'Baldur,' I shouted with all the strength my lungs could

muster. Again: 'Baldur.'

He arrived within moments, closing the door behind him. 'What is it?'

I was propped against the side of the bed, my elbows sticking out and my legs splayed haphazardly.

'I need your help. I need photographs and maps of lakes. Crater lakes – dead volcanoes, or even living ones. Any that are filled with water. All that you can find. Can you do that?'

'Of course, I'll get people on it at once. Are you okay?'

'I'm fine Baldur.'

'Shall I have food brought?'

'Food?' I had to think for a few moments. The idea confused me. My heart was still racing. 'Yes. I shall eat.'

'The Mathematikoi are eager to see you.'

'I shall see each one individually. Pass on the instruction to find the photographs then come back. I will tell you what I think, then meet the Mathematikoi. You must hurry, Baldur.'

'Indeed I shall.'

He left without asking the first question I would have thought of in his position – Why? A Mathematikoi knew when to act and when to ask questions. When he returned I told him what I had rediscovered: the Earth, like other celestial objects, is a concentration of matter, and thus a concentrated manifestation of the Aumic boom that gave birth to everything we see and feel. Our planet is like a battery, gathering in and storing up the creative force that binds everything and triggers the evolution of inert matter into more complex forms. Compared to the muted hum of the lifeless planets and the near-silence of space, our tiny planet roars with it. But the Earth, like everything else that exists, has inherent instabilities. When the tensions become too great, violent bursts of energy are flung from its core to compensate.

Sonic screams hurtle from natural vents in the mantle and rock the planet at frequencies we can neither hear nor even sense as vibrations. As the highest form of evolution, the human mind is the most intricate of all harmonic structures, the pinnacle of creative achievement, but without the benefit of many lifetimes of focus and training, even we are insensible to it. The howl is nullified in the emptiness of space. This is *the event*, and it happens periodically on vast geological timescales. I hadn't known this an hour earlier. Windows were opening in my mind.

'It will happen soon, Baldur, and we must be ready.' I knew that it was essential for me to be close to the vent when it occurred, but not why. The only clue to its whereabouts was in Thon's final words, and I trusted him. If the lake he had mentioned was in the crater of a volcano, then the deep channel of cooled magma that reached down through the mantle could feasibly act as a funnel or a horn, channelling the force outwards. The event would be like a planetary 'Aumic hiccup'. It was a long shot, but with the information I had, it was the best conclusion I could draw. I was encouraged by how comfortable the theory felt. Most of my life had been defined by a pervading sense of déjà vu and I had always trusted thoughts that felt familiar.

Baldur accepted what I said, but raised questions about the reliability of Thon's reference to the lake. He did so in a tactful way, but I felt certain he was aggrieved to find me taking counsel from anyone who was not Mathematikoi. There was nothing I could say to assuage his fears, other than the honest truth: I believed in Thon's testimony. After all, he was the one who had found me and facilitated my awakening.

That afternoon I started meeting the Mathematikoi. I spent time with each, discussing the research they had carried out in my absence and telling them some of what I had learnt recently. At times I felt a little lost as my mind slipped back into the persona of Sebastian, the relatively young man in his late twenties, hopelessly out of his depth in the company of such learned men. But they did not see Sebastian. They saw 'The Master', a term I no longer felt comfortable with.

I found the developments in their research fascinating, but was dismayed by their focus on the structure and form of instrumental sound. Like Thon, many of them failed to realise instrumental music could only deliver solace, temporary joy and mere glimpses of the second repetition. Its true purpose was to trigger the circuits of the mind that facilitated greater understanding. The Mathematikoi tore themselves apart over the Comma and grew frustrated when perfection eluded them. If a 'divine being' had invoked the force of creation to ask itself a question, and if humans were the ineffable mechanisms that were destined to solve the riddle, then a sense of perfection and an affinity for the mysteries of harmony were the best clues we had been given. The combination of euphoria and nostalgia that music provokes in our souls is a vital gift, but only a pointer to something greater. Music is a reminder that we are blessed with an ability to seek out the transcendent, to grasp for understanding, to fashion ideals, to admire beauty, to one day solve the riddle and return to the heart of the divine, eventually to be subsumed in a perpetual state of absolute harmony.

The next day Baldur brought the first batch of photographs and maps, but none of them triggered a memory or shed any light on the mystery. I decided to introduce a semblance of routine into my lifestyle, a welcome change from the chaos of the preceding weeks. In the mornings I met individual Mathematikoi in their rooms. As I went from room to room, I was surprised how big the monastery was. The corridors seemed endless. At noon each day I looked through the latest batch of photographs and maps which Baldur had provided. In the afternoons I stayed in my room, practising meditation and spending progressively more and more time in the rarefied state of the third repetition. Every so often I knelt on the floor to sense the vibrations that ricocheted through the mantle and reverberated around the hard crust of the earth through my fingertips, evoking a tremulous sensation at the base of my skull. The sensations became more familiar with every passing day, and I learnt how to diminish the strain they put on my body. I found myself growing more and more detached from the world – spending my waking hours in a daze, but still able to listen and respond intelligently. I was living in a perpetual state of awareness, my mind open and free from noise. In the evenings I fell asleep early and the only dream I ever had was a recurring image of golden light, the image of the Aum, trembling in a lake of crystal blue water beneath a yellow sun.

A week went by and I was no closer to solving the riddle, but in the meantime I was utterly at peace, enjoying the company of the Mathematikoi and revelling in the thrilling landscapes of my meditations. On the eighth day, I was interrupted in the afternoon by a knock on the door. I had told Baldur to avoid disturbing me during the time I had put aside for meditation, so I was surprised by the distant tapping of knuckle on wood. It took me a few moments to realise what it was and a few more to open my eyes and respond.

'Come in, Baldur.' Nobody else would knock on my door in those precious afternoon hours. 'What is it?'

'There is somebody here who wishes to see you. I've told her that you are unavailable, but she's very insistent.'

'Who is she?'

'She hasn't given a name. She says she's travelled a long way. She says she knows you.'

'What does she want?'

'She won't say. She refuses to leave until she's seen you. She gave me this.' He handed me a small envelope. I opened it carefully and took out a folded piece of paper. It was old, worn and delicate, but I managed to unfold it without tearing the paper. The handwriting was faded but readable. I recognised it. Baldur stood in curious anticipation as I read the lines.

> *When we think of music, how it reaches to the height of heaven and embraces the earth; how there is in it communication with the spirit-like processes of nature, we must pronounce its height the highest, its reach the furthest, its depth the most profound, its breadth the greatest. When one has mastered completely the principles of music, the natural, gentle and honest heart is easily developed, and with this development comes joy. This joy merges in a feeling of repose. The man in this constant repose becomes heaven-like, his actions spirit-like. So it is when mastering music.*
>
> *Yao Chi*

The handwriting was mine.

'Bring her to me, Baldur, and ask Noi to bring refreshments.' As far as I knew, the Mathematikoi were the only people who knew where I was, so the fact that somebody else had found me was remarkable.

Noi delivered a jug of aromatic water and left. I poured two glasses and placed the jug on the floor next to the table. A few moments later a tall woman with long silver hair appeared. She stood for a few moments, her eyes fixed on mine, her breath gentle and slow. I was amazed at the contrast between her apparent age, and the health and vitality that radiated from her. Her eyes were green, vibrant and daunting. Her hair shimmered in the light. I stood up to offer her a chair, and was instantly aware she was watching every movement I made.

'Are you Sebastian?'

'I am. Do I know you?'

'Do you recognise me?'

'I'm afraid I don't.'

She said nothing, continuing to study me in silence. I offered her the chair again, and she took it. I crossed the room, closed the door and returned to my seat. I offered her one of the glasses of water which she accepted graciously but left untouched. The piece of paper and its envelope lay on the table between us.

'Tell me, when you were born?' She asked.

'I beg your pardon.'

'When were you born, Sebastian?'

I couldn't see any harm in answering, so I told her. She studied me closely. I held her gaze. 'Have you come for a reason?' I placed my finger on the piece of paper.

'I have come to help you, if you are who I think you are.'

'Who do you think I am?'

'A friend. From long ago. When I was a young girl, I knew an old man. We were close friends. He told me his secrets. I kept them for him. He told me to find him and return them.'

'Where did he go?'

'He died, then he slept for a while in the spirit world, as we all do. He slept for a long time, waiting, or perhaps lost.'

'And then?'

'The world took hold of his spirit and brought it back. It gave him new life.'

'What did you call this man?'

'Pilan. It was a name we gave him.'

The name was unfamiliar. I never remembered names.

'Do you recognise me?' I asked.

'You are very different, but your eyes are the same, your spirit is the same, you have the same soul. It is you.' A small tear crept out of her eye and sparkled in the light.

I recognised her. 'I was Pilan.'

'You were.'

'How did you find me?'

'The shaman remembered you. He often passed into the spirit world to look for you. His son told me where I could find you. I have waited a long time. I nearly gave up hope, but I had to live because I had your secrets and I couldn't pass them to anyone else. When you left us, your friends stayed. One of them would always stay behind when the others went away. But this time, they all went and I knew there was a gathering; I knew the time had come to look for you. I went to the shaman's son and asked him to find you.'

'My friends?'

'The Sufis. I saw one of them in the hall outside.'

'A Mathematikoi?'

'I don't know that word. Their faces are different, but they have the same spirit. They lived in the buildings that had the mark on the door. They weren't with you when you passed away, but they came to see your body afterwards.'

'And you said they were Sufis.'

'That's what you were, too. You played the vina, you taught us the art of ecstatic whirling and you taught us the wisdom of the Sufi mystics: Rumi, Kulliyyat, Iraqi and Qunawi.'

'I don't remember.'

'The life immediately prior to that which you are leading is always the most difficult to recall. That's why the Brotherhood is so important for you.' She closed her eyes, whispered the name 'Rumi' and then spoke words that were obviously his:

> *'I died as a mineral and became a plant*
> *I died as a plant and became an animal*
> *I died as an animal and became a man. Why should I fear?*
> *When did I ever become less through dying?*
> *Next time I will die to human nature*
> *Spreading my wings and lifting up my head with the angels*
> *Then I will jump the streams of angelic nature*
> *I will become what does not enter the imagination*
> *I will become nothing, for non-existence plays The Tune.'*

Her eyes opened and she smiled. Rumi's words had been surprisingly familiar. As she had spoken each line, the succeeding one had materialised in my mind. They triggered memories of other passages I had read, or maybe written, in the past. I felt close to them, as if they were my own. I listened carefully as she spoke again, reciting the lines of another, so familiar, piece:

> *'Philosophers say that we've taken*
> *These melodies from the revolution of the spheres*
> *The songs people sing with lute and throat*
> *Are the sounds of the spheres in their turning...*
> *We heard those melodies in paradise*
> *Water and clay have covered us in doubt*
> *But we still remember something of those tunes.*
> *Music is the food of lovers –*
> *Within it they find the image of union.'*

She sat quietly as lines of ancient verse drifted in and out of my mind.

'What was I called? Before your tribe gave me the name Pilan.'

'I don't remember. My name for you was Innie.'

The name meant no more to me than Pilan had. They were both forgotten.

'And I gave you this?' I held up her note. The dry paper crinkled between us.

'You told me it would catch your attention, in case you couldn't remember. I have come to give you back your secrets.'

'My secrets?'

'I know that you must listen to the song of the earth. Do you remember these words: *Each atom is a word, each word speaks a name, each name has a different tongue, and each tongue has a song?*'

'Yes.'

A shiver ran up my spine.

'I know that the earth will soon call out to the spirit world, creating a bridge, if you choose to use it. Do you know this?'

'Yes.'

The words she had quoted were not in my own style. I had couched them in terms that suited her culture. I was trembling with anticipation.

'I know where the lake is.'

And there it was, like a crash of lightning.

'And I know when you must go.'

I wanted to reach out and clasp her in my arms.

'Where is it?'

'Sumatra. You must be there three weeks from now. It is called Maninjau, Danau Maninjau.'

'Three weeks! Maninjau. Yes, Maninjau.'

I darted across the room and pulled at the door. As it opened, Noi fell forward, his cheeks reddening. He'd been listening, but I didn't mind his curiosity. I told him to hurry to Baldur and ask him to fetch maps of Danau Maninjau, in

Sumatra. I must have seen them before amongst all the others, but they hadn't sparked any recognition. I closed the door and returned to my chair.

'You are Chenoa.'

'Yes.'

'I remember.'

I asked her to tell me about her life. It felt strange. I remembered her name, I remembered who she was, but very little of the emotional bond that must have existed between us remained. It always happened like this. I spared a thought for Noi. He could one day be in the same position with his own father. The burden of the Mathematikoi was a heavy one. My heart swelled with affection for them.

Chenoa told me very little about her own life, but she did tell me about my life as Pilan. A man from her village had fallen ill with fever and was close to death. The disease should not have been fatal but the man's will was weak, his strength was drained and he was losing the battle for life. According to her Native American traditions medicinal songs were received by the shamans as gifts in dreams. The shaman passed into the spirit world and slept, but instead of receiving a song, he was told of the impending arrival of a traveller seeking refuge. When I arrived shortly afterwards, the shaman welcomed me and asked for assistance in curing the stricken man. I played music at his bedside for a day and night. Another day passed in silence and the tribe grew anxious, but the shaman refused to allow anyone to enter while I was there. Another day passed and the sick man emerged, weak, but alive, while I slept for a further two days. The stricken man was Chenoa's father.

She was young at the time and I was already an old man, but a fondness developed between us as she nursed me through old age. I spent most of my time alone. Chenoa remembered me sitting quietly by the old pine trees, eyelids fluttering as if caught on a breeze. Sometimes I sang with the tribe, and they often called on my help when people were sick. It was said that I could control my dreams and summon spirit-songs at will. When Chenoa was eighteen years old, I became ill with a fever that neither I nor the shaman could cure. On my deathbed, I asked for Chenoa and told her my secrets. Pilan passed away shortly after, taking all the memories I had of his life with him. When my eyes opened again, I was Sebastian.

Several times over the years she had left to search me out, but the expeditions had always proved futile. As old age swept over her, she had become progressively more anxious and fearful she had failed me. Facing the imminence of her own death, she sought the assistance of the current shaman, the son of the shaman I had known when I was Pilan. He went into the wilderness for two days, then came back and gave her a name: Sebastian; a place: Chiang Mai; and a sketch of a building: Baldur's monastery. She set out immediately. But now, she said, her spirit had no reason to hold on to a worn-out body; she would not live much longer and was eager to return to her home as quickly as possible.

I longed to know her, to remember fully who she was and who I had been, but accepted that she must return home before the shadow of death reached her. She had held my secrets for many anxious years, but I could barely remember the affection I must have once felt for her.

She must have read my thoughts. 'I never expected you to know who I was. In moments of hope I thought I'd find you and you'd look just the same as I remembered you, but they were the dreams of a young girl. Now I am an old woman, but my spirit is still young. You are a young man and your spirit is old. It is time for me to die and for you to find peace. I won't hug you because we are not the same people we were years ago. But maybe our spirits will meet again and we will remember. Perhaps you will be an old man, and I will be a little girl and we won't have to feel sad because our memories are not so good.'

A knock came at the door and Baldur entered with the photographs of Maninjau. Chenoa asked me if there was a room where she could rest. She had to catch a flight to Bangkok early the next morning. I told Baldur to arrange everything and take care of her. I looked deeply into Chenoa's eyes for a few moments. She left without saying another word. Baldur followed her and I was left alone with the maps. I took the biggest one I could find in the pile and held it up to the light with anticipation. It was an aerial photograph of a small crater, perhaps eight or nine kilometres across. The rim was relatively steep, its upper levels dense with tropical foliage and the lowland areas scattered with a network of rice paddies and barely visible buildings. A few jetties stretched out into the lake, which was almost circular. The crater was conspicuous because the height of the rim was uniform, except for a great triangular cleft on the east side. I turned the photograph over in my hands and on the back there was a simple inscription: Danau Maninjau, Sumatra. I had found it. I'd known it all along, but amongst the centuries of dormant memory, I had somehow lost the most vital part. If it weren't for a Native American girl who had stepped out of one life and into another to help me, I would never have known.

I lay on the bed and marvelled at the convolution of my life. I recalled all the people I had encountered in the last year, each of them adding some piece to the puzzle. My work was nearly over. There was nothing left to do except reach the lake in three weeks, a task that should be free of complications as it was normally only a week's journey. I wasn't sure what would happen when I arrived, but I felt certain it would be an ending, a resolution. Whatever happened, I knew I would not return to the Brotherhood

There was still one important task remaining: I had to supervise my departure from the Mathematikoi. I had to leave them with a full knowledge of everything that had happened; no more secrets. I resolved to gather my notebooks and my dream journals and complete them with another document that I would write in the time remaining. I would leave them with Baldur to be used as references or to be compiled into one story: the story of the Brotherhood, of the Mathematikoi; the true story of a man known by many names, but who would now be remembered properly as Pythagoras.

My routine changed. I began my meditations before dawn and stopped at lunchtime. In the afternoon I wrote, and in the evenings I spent time with the Mathematikoi, leading them in group meditation or holding discussions about the nature of the repetitions, the theories of sound and music or any other topics they chose to raise.

I recalled the Semicircle of Samos and the secret meetings we held in the nearby cave. I was overcome with nostalgia and lifted by the joy that accompanies the rare blessing of ancient companionship. Our name was suited to our nature – the Brotherhood – though many of the Mathematikoi were in fact women. I spoke at length with the Mathematikoi about what would happen after I journeyed to the lake. They would need to reassess their objectives. Changes were inevitable. I had hoped that my departure would free them from their obligations, but they seemed intent on continuing my work. I told them that there should be no more secrets; that the truth about us should be told to anyone who asked. A few resisted, but the end of our secrecy was inevitable. I told them to follow their instincts and consider the options carefully and democratically. The choices were theirs to make now, not mine.

It was in such conversations that another unanswered question sprang to my mind: why had I left the most important piece of information in the hands of a young girl and not the Mathematikoi? She had found me with only three weeks to spare after spending many years looking. The Mathematikoi had centuries of experience in tracking me down and were far more likely to catch up with me in time, though even they had left it perilously close. I was still a young man, and I suppose things had moved far more quickly in this lifetime than they ever had before. I had forced myself into ascendancy, knocking at the door of Sebastian's mind as he slept, pushing my way through at a dangerous pace, which explained why I had been so exhausted so often. But why Chenoa? I summoned Baldur, but he was equally perplexed.

'What do you think will happen to the Brotherhood if I leave and never return?'

'What?'

'What do you think will happen? If my work was finished and I never came back, how would it change? What would it become?'

'I'm not sure.'

'It would continue?'

'Yes.'

'Have you spoken with the others about it?'

'To some, yes.'

'And?'

'Their emotions are mixed; their instincts divided. I see fear in some eyes, sadness in others, pragmatism in most, but no joy, no excitement at the prospect. We've endured a long time. We have a strong sense of identity. We risk losing it.'

'I have no choice in this matter Baldur. I am tired, drained. I am finished here. When I leave this time, I will not return.'

'I know.'

'You will have a full account, I'll make certain of it. There will be nothing left for me to teach.'

'I know.'

'I want you to travel with me. You and I alone.'

'Of course.'

'I want you to announce a date for our departure. We shall leave two days before on the pretence of some other business – a trip to Doi Inthanon or a meeting with Ch'ien. Will you do that?'

'Of course, but…'

'I want to go quietly, without fuss or distractions.'

'What will happen at the lake?'

'I've no idea Baldur, but I intend to go there and find out. I'm relying on you to help me.'

This was one of the last cogent discussions I had with anyone. I was finding it increasingly difficult to concentrate on conversations. I struggled to keep my mind focussed and often I'd begin a sentence and lose track of it before I'd finished. Baldur had realised the conversation had exhausted me as he rose from his chair, gripped my shoulder and left the room, his face solemn. From that point on he subtly reduced the time I had to spend with the others and I was able to save my strength for the journey ahead. As a result I spent progressively more and more time alone in my room, meditating deeply, my mind racing to the rhythm and melody of the ethereal *musica mundana*. I barely noticed the change, but I was now almost permanently consumed by the sensations that had so affected me in Ch'ien's cave many months before.

By the time Baldur and I left the monastery, I was able to sustain myself for several hours in the rarefied state of the third repetition without suffering the trauma of dislocation. I felt the restless vibrations of the earth without the need to prostrate myself on the floor. I felt them continuously, as a constant nausea that kept me from sleeping. But I no longer needed sleep. I barely ate. I drank six or seven litres of water a day. I sustained my strength and I no longer felt the need for rest.

On the final evening, I held a group meditation with the Mathematikoi. I led them in a chant. The room reverberated with a hundred ancient voices. The sounds hummed in the air for a while, then the entire gathering drifted into the second repetition together and the air became silent. A crimson light streamed around us. I felt the tremors of the earth rushing through me. When I opened my eyes, I saw a multitude of eyes aglow with the same thrill I had felt the first time *musica mundana* had washed over me. Every face was smiling, flushed with vitality. There was a sense of contentment in that room that nothing could sully. I wished the walls would fall away so the whole world could join us. The meditation lasted for several hours before I drew it to an end. The Mathematikoi stayed for a while and talked, and then gradually dispersed to their beds. I spoke to each one as they left, wishing them well and saying goodnight with affection, though it was in fact, goodbye. Baldur and I were leaving early in the morning and I wouldn't see them again. I felt sad, but I knew that it was necessary to break ties and leave without looking back. I spent the entire evening in motion, the pulse of the earth growing more and more restless as each hour passed.

Maninjau

I can barely remember the details of the journey to Sumatra. I had told Baldur to avoid aeroplanes because I wanted to stay close to the ground. It wasn't safe for me to drive because I couldn't concentrate, so he drove us the full length of Thailand, stopping only every five or six hours for essential rests. Our first stop was at the old city of Sukhothai. I sat beneath the tall trees where I had first noticed the loss of my necklace, an age ago. I thought of Thon, Kun and Ch'ien for the last time.

A day and night passed quickly and before I knew it we had crossed the Malaysian border and were taking the ferry to George Town. I sought out the engraver's shop, asking Baldur if he knew what had become of him. He couldn't tell me, and was surprised when I told him how the old man had helped me to find the Brotherhood. Perhaps I'd imagined him, conjuring his words from the recesses of my mind to trigger the first essential steps to wakefulness. Everything I had ever known was turning into echoes and dying away on the wind. An hour later we were on the boat to Medan, and several hours later, in Sumatra. Baldur hired a Landrover and we continued our journey through the vast and beautiful island. Looking out of the window, I was struck by the endless rows of identical trees, neatly arranged in straight lines. The forests had been tamed, turned into tree farms.

The closer we got to the crater, the more oblivious I became to the world around me. On one occasion I broke from my reflections and was unable to recognise Baldur. When I tried to speak, my words were incoherent. I was entirely dependent on him.

We stopped at a small village near Danau Toba. Baldur slept. I couldn't. I sat at a roadside cafe listening to the cicadas. On the other side of the street an old man was playing a batak mandolin, surrounded by friends and what seemed like a hundred yapping puppies. They were so many canine voices singing with him that they formed a drone over which the tinkling melody danced. I looked into the eyes of the audience. They were smiling. While the music played, they had no concerns.

That is one of the last clear memories I have of the world. Giant trees hung over us. The moon was silver. The earth was rumbling. Baldur put his hand on my shoulder and we set out again, heading south towards Maninjau.

By the time we reached the slopes of the crater, it felt as if the rhythms of *musica mundana* had become audible, and I was deafened. I could no longer hear Baldur when he spoke to me. We left the Landrover and took the path up to the rim of the crater on foot. I needed Baldur's support, and it took a long time, but eventually we cleared the summit of the rim and the lake spread before us like a bowl of mercury shimmering in the light of dawn. The sun rose through the triangular cleft on the east side. The light was stunning. Baldur pointed at the lake and I saw a shape in the water. The surface was rippling, but the waves were not moving. I could barely stand. My vision blurred. I reached out for Baldur's arm, and it began.

I'm rolling down the crater rim, crashing through dense jungle, groves of magnificent bamboo passing in a flurry as I tumble towards the lakeshore. The sun has crept over the crater's edge. The beguiling burble of a nearby stream ushers me forward. Everything is moving so quickly.

I hit the road and freeze, numbed. Somebody is standing next to me. He pushes me forward and we head along the snake-like twists and turns, passing through waking villages and sleepy fields, eventually arriving at the shore of the lake. The waves lap gently at my feet. The ripples scatter the morning sun. A fish darts effortlessly through the lucid fluid. Its movement is music.

I'm walking down a jetty. The light is strong and the crater glows with a sweet crimson hue. The air thins and becomes moist. I sit alone at the end of the pier. I close my eyes. The sound of water on wood surrounds me, invades me and slows the world down. The music is everywhere: inside me, in the water, in the air, deep in the earth. I focus, I listen, I am overwhelmed.

I am in a canoe. Somebody is with me, propelling it. We paddle to the centre of the lake, through tall waves that don't move. They make me shiver, I am trembling. Who am I? I am Pythagoras. Where am I? I am at the end of my journey.

I rise. I am alone, standing precariously in the swaying hollow of carved wood. An oar is floating in the water. It drifts away from the canoe. The shattered reflection of the blue sky dances on the water. I turn my head upward and the mountain roars. I let out a cry I cannot hear. Never has the ocean of the sky felt so close; I can see stars through the daylight. A bird of prey swoops from a dizzying height. A raging symphony consumes the world. Another roar. It shakes my soul and I see light streaming upwards. I bend my knees, breathe deeply and leap into the air. For a moment I freeze in time, arms outstretched.

Two thousand years disintegrate in my mind. I have forgotten who I am and why I am here. The pitch of the world rises and the universe begins to turn around me once more. I crash like thunder through the surface and race downward. The pressure increases. Darkness engulfs me; quiet stillness; phenomenal noise. I cease to breathe. My lungs fill with water and my body does not resist, I do not feel its pain. The tempo slows: flashes of light, melodies, ephemeral crystals of music. My body has gone. Brilliant shades of crimson fire; raw energy.

Then, silence. The entire spectrum of universal noise concordant in one soul. Devouring harmony. No history; no future. Thoughts are shadows. The laughter of atoms. The weeping of stars. Sound, like a focussed beam of light. The primeval tone. I have passed from the realm of life and death.

I am become music.